At the Sign of the Star

At the Sign of the Star

KATHERINE STURTEVANT

A SUNBURST BOOK

FARRAR STRAUS GIROUX

For my mother, Lee Sturtevant,
who always provided me with the very best books—
and with anything else I wanted to read

Copyright © 2000 by Katherine Sturtevant
All rights reserved
Distributed in Canada by Douglas & McIntyre Ltd.
Printed in the United States of America
First edition, 2000
Sunburst edition, 2002
3 5 7 9 10 8 6 4

Library of Congress Cataloging-in-Publication Data
Sturtevant, Katherine.
    At the sign of the star / Katherine Sturtevant.— 1st ed.
      p. cm.
    Summary: In seventeenth-century London, Meg, who has little interest in
cooking, needlework, or other homemaking classes for girls, dreams of becoming
a bookseller and someday inheriting her father's book store.
    ISBN-13: 978-0-374-40458-1 (pbk.)
    ISBN-10: 0-374-40458-5 (pbk.)
    1. London (England)—History—17th century—Juvenile fiction. [1. London
(England)—History—17th century—Fiction. 2. Great Britain—History—1660–1714
—Fiction. 3. Sex role—Fiction. 4. Booksellers and bookselling—Fiction.] I. Title.

PZ7.S94127 At 2000
[Fic]—dc21

                                                              00-20448

At the Sign of the Star

NEWS FROM THE STARS
Almanac for the Year of Christ 1677

I was with Hester when we saw the comet in the night sky over London, saw it before anyone spoke of it or wondered what it meant. It was just past midnight on an April evening, a week or more past Easter. My father had come home late from being in company, and I was anxious to hear if the playwright John Dryden had been there, or perhaps Aphra Behn, London's female playwright. Hester and I waited up in the parlor, as we often did, thinking to have a mug of ale with him while he shared his gossip. But he told me Dryden wasn't there, and when I asked who was, he only smiled at me and winked, and said it was none of my affair.

Then he went into the small parlor to read manuscripts by candlelight, and Hester and I went to our room. But before we undid our stays we both decided we were not sleepy, and agreed that the spring air felt fresh and fine. So it was that we ended up sitting out of doors on the step, looking into the lane that ran behind the house. We sat with the kitchen door held open so that we might dash within if a cutthroat should come suddenly upon us. This was my own precaution. Hester was careless of such matters, and said I ought to have been named Prudence instead of Margaret. But I am no Puritan to bear such a name as that, and am satisfied to be called instead after saints and noblewomen. Margaret is my name, and I am called Meg.

"My father is not himself," I said to Hester as we sat peering into the darkness. "What bothers him, do you think?"

"Why, nothing bothers him. Think how cheerful he was over the counter this morning, when Mrs. Beckwith and her daughter came in."

"That means nothing. 'Tis part of his job, to laugh with those who buy his books."

"He has been in fine humor," Hester observed.

"Too fine. He is almost foolish. He is trying to make up his mind about something, and seeks to hide from me while he does it."

"About whether to publish Mr. Coles's Latin and English dictionary, that is all."

"Nay, it is something bigger."

"You make too much of little things. Are your feelings hurt, that he chose not to answer a girl's prying questions when bedtime was long past?"

She meant to affront me, for the fun of it, so I stayed

sulky and silent to please her. We both gazed at the night. It was full dark, for the moon had set, or had not yet risen, and we had no lantern in our street. I counted three candles in the windows across the street from us. I heard the rattle of a laundry tub from the house of Mr. Grove, who lived next door, for the laundress was beginning her night work. Soon after I heard the bell of the watchman as he made his rounds. There was the smell of rosemary nearby—Cook grew it under the window.

"With whom did he sup?" I wondered aloud after a little, but Hester spoke at the same moment.

"Why, look at that, Meg," she said, and pointed upward with her long arm.

I gazed up so mightily it made my eyes sting, and there saw a star with a fiery wake, as though a chariot had flown through the dark heavens and parted them behind. " 'Tis a comet," I said.

"Surely not."

"I'm certain of it. Sir Henry has described them to me, he saw one five years ago."

"God protect us," Hester said in a grave voice. "What can it foretell for us?"

I shook my head doubtfully.

"Perhaps another great fire will consume the City," she said.

"Perhaps the Plague will return," I offered.

"Or the Dutch will sail up the Thames once more and will murder us in our beds."

"Or the drought will come and the crops will fail."

"Or the King may die without an heir."

It was my turn to think of a calamity, but I could think of none. Instead I said, "Sir Henry says that we see the same stars as folk in foreign lands. So they are seeing this selfsame comet. Perhaps misfortune is meant for some other country. Perhaps it is the French who will suffer. Or the Spanish. Perhaps it is the people in the colonies, across the sea."

"I never heard such nonsense," Hester said. "The people in the colonies can worry about their own misfortunes; we must worry about ours. A comet is a sign from God that terrible things will befall us all unless we mend our ways. And what is less likely than London Town mending her ways?"

Hester was from the countryside in Surrey and had no very great opinion of London. She was both cousin and maidservant, and in those months lived with my father and me at the sign of the Star, where we sold the books my father published, and other books as well. She was then sixteen, four years older than I, and was to marry Thomas Whitcombe, from her village, someday.

I stared up at the comet. I knew it was moving, though it seemed still as stone. I wondered what it really meant, for London, and for me. "London isn't so very bad," I said, not because I thought so but to make Hester fire up. "What ways ought she to mend?"

"Ha!" was all Hester said.

"I'm sure *I'm* pious enough."

"You! Is that why you sit reading almanacs and plays, instead of sermons and psalmbooks as you ought?"

This was an old argument—old and comfortable as slippers. It was I who taught Hester to read in the first place, but she made no more use of it than to peer into Bibles and recipe books. She didn't mind, though, when I sat on a stool in the kitchen and read stories to her of Robin Hood or Long Meg, while she rolled out the dough for tarts.

"I don't mind a sermon, if it's nicely argued," I answered Hester.

"I'm sure God's grateful to you for that!"

"But I can't think why Father has taken to going to St. Botolph's of late. Reverend Little is so dull!"

"I'm sure your father has his reasons."

"The choir's fine. Do you think it's the hymns he likes?"

"Ask him, if you want so much to know."

"I did, but he just laughed and said that I am curious as a cat. He's not himself, Hester."

"This again," she answered.

We sat a few minutes more, and heard the watch call the hour.

"We'll go in now, or you'll get the chill," Hester said. Every once in a while she thinks she's my mother instead of my servant. But she's nothing like my mother was, nothing.

❧ 2 ❧

I was eight when my mother died. She died in childbirth, of course. Of course. Almost every year her big belly grew yet bigger, and each time she bore me a wee brother or sister. First was Christopher—he died three weeks after his birthday; I was too young to remember him. Then Frances, who died at four months. I remember her, I think. That is, I remember a baby in the house for a few days, before she was sent to the country to nurse. I must have been three, then.

Next came Louis. Louis I remember well. He was born when my father's fortunes were low, and there was no money for a wet nurse, so he lived with us and sucked his milk from my mother's breasts. I changed his fouled clouts when he was but a babe, and spooned pap into his mouth while he stood in his standing stool, and it was I who taught him to drink his ale from a cup after he was weaned. Louis grew to be three years old, and was such a brother as no girl ever had. He loved to hang on my apron and listen to my stories. He begged me to teach him to read, though he was such a little thing, and could not yet remember his *A* and his *B*. My mother would laugh to see us together.

When I was seven I caught a fever, and Louis caught it, too, and my father and mother as well. The doctor purged us and bled us and gave us foul remedies to drink, and at last we did recover, except Louis.

The house was a quiet one after he died, and when my mother conceived once more I was glad of it, hoping to hear a brother's laughter soon again. But my last sister died in the bearing, yet unnamed, and my mother died with her.

One afternoon in the months of mourning that followed my mother's death, my father came into the kitchen as I sat there chopping turnips with Cook.

"Who will teach her?" he said, as though speaking to himself.

"I already know how to read, Papa," I answered him.

"That is the littlest thing you must know. What of cookery and healing and minding the household? What of needlework and French? You must be sent away to school."

I laid my knife to one side. "Will they teach me Latin and Greek?" I asked.

"Nay, Meg. Those studies are for boys."

"Will they teach me the stationers' trade, so that I may help you and Robert in the shop?" Robert was my father's chief apprentice.

He smiled. "No, Meg. But they will teach you piety and gentleness."

"I do not want to go to school."

"It is not for you to choose, Margaret. You cannot spend your days sitting in the kitchen, chopping turnips like a serving girl."

That was when Cook spoke. She sat opposite me at the table, pulling and punching at the dough that would cover our sparrow pie at supper. Her hands were covered with flour, and flour scattered across the thick slices of turnip I had cut with such care. "It's only that she might not be idle, sir. She hasn't the spirit to be much alone since her mother died, poor thing," Cook said, and shook her head at me. Her name was Mary, I think. She was a thin, worrying woman who made wonderful stews. The cook we have now does not make such savory stews.

"Her loss is less than mine," my father answered her.

It made me angry, because he always had more of her when she lived, and now he claimed more of her when she was dead as well. I looked up at him, and he looked straight back at me. I knew that he saw the anger in my eyes.

"You had your mother for eight years," he said. "Many children do not have their mothers as long."

I have thought often about those words. They have made me long to remember every moment of those eight years. But of my infancy and young years I remember nothing, and later I was often with Louis instead of my mother. Some things I do remember. I remember that my mother was kind—kind to servants, kind to beggars. I remember that she was clever. She read as often as my father, and argued with him about what ought to be printed. It was she who taught me to read. I remember that she was stout, and loved the color blue. That her feet ached often, which sometimes made her tongue sharp with me and with Louis. But she loved my father, and when arguing with him she would leave off in the middle of an angry sentence and shake her head, and thank God for him instead.

I had her for eight years, but I wish I had had her longer, or at least more often while she lived. I know not why she died—how God gained by it, I mean. I do not know, either, why I am the only one of her children who lived. I often ponder it.

To my father I said only, "Yes, sir."

"Are you happy, then, chopping turnips in the kitchen?"

"Yes, sir," I said, still determined that he would not send me to school.

"You are my heir, Margaret," he said. "Someday all my books will be yours, and my copyrights, and my other interests as well. With such a dowry you need not trouble yourself about marrying an old man nor a sour one. You may choose someone in the trade, if you like, and be a partner to him as your mother was to me. But you must first fit yourself to be mistress of the household you will one day govern. You must go to school."

He turned and left. I raised my knife and began chopping once more, carefully, for even then I was a careful girl. When I finished, the turnip was in tatters.

"La, Meg, what are you doing?" Mary scolded, and cuffed me with a floury hand.

"I have remembered something I must tell my father," I said, and put the knife down upon the table.

I found him in the shop, which was not open. "Please,

Papa, you must not send me to school," I said. "For how can I there learn the trade? I must help in the shop, like Robert."

In the end I won him over. He said he would find someone to teach me at home, and from time to time he did, but my teachers were not very suitable and did not stay long. From one I learned to cast accounts, and from another to make plague-water to ward off infection.

But in the main I worked, helping my father at our shop where it stood in Little Britain, a street crowded with booksellers. As I worked I listened to the great men who gathered there as soot gathers on a chimney piece. Perhaps, as I once heard my father say, our shillings came more from sermons and Latin grammars than from poetry and plays. But being the friend and publisher of John Dryden, the greatest of London's great literary men, played no small part in making my father an important man. As I grew I saw much of plump, rosy Mr. Dryden. At first I cared only that he was kindly, and free with a playful jest, but later I began to hear him when he defended the plays of Shakespeare or the rhymed couplet. Still later I read his plays, both the comedies and the tragedies, and some of his verses. And when Hester worried over my education I told her that it did not matter, for I was learning all I needed to know from my father, and the company he kept, and from the books we sold at the sign of the Star.

At breakfast, Hester and I told my father of the comet, and he was almost angry.

"How would you know a comet?" he asked. "Are you an astrologer now? You must be mistaken."

"You'll see soon enough, when all London is talking of it," I said, angry in my turn. I set my tankard down with a thump, and a few drops spilled onto the wooden trencher that held my bread and butter. "Then you will admit I'm right about something, at last."

"Stop talking nonsense, Daughter. A comet's a larger matter than whether a child is right or wrong about something. What can it mean?" He went on, almost to himself. "Does it mean the year is not auspicious?"

"Not auspicious for what?" I asked, but he ignored me, and I thought his face looked worried in the flicker of the tallow candles. The parlor had a large window, but it was westward looking and the weak dawn light had not yet reached it.

"What do the almanacs say?" Hester asked as she handed round the oatcake. I believe she hoped to distract us both.

"Andrews's almanac, *News from the Stars*, says there is an unusually long transit of Mars through Cancer this year," I answered. "With *many* animosities in April."

"Andrews means there will be conflicts between nations," my father said.

"*And* storms. *And* losses to pirates."

"How is it that you find the time to read through every book and broadside upon our shelves?" he asked.

"Cold beef?" Hester offered.

"I suppose if it is worth printing it is worth reading," I said.

"I doubt it's worth printing. Next year I'll not undertake it."

This was indeed unlike him. I stared at him as though by doing so I could divine the excess of choler or phlegm that had caused his strange humor, but all I saw was my father: long of face, square of chin, pink of cheek—exactly like myself. His gray hair was awry. He never put on his wig until after breakfast.

At last I ventured to say, "But, Father, you must publish an almanac! We sell so many!"

"Oh, that is the measure of worth, is it?"

"If you like Barker's better . . . "

"Barker is a charlatan," my father said, scowling.

"Why, you yourself have consulted him often," I said in surprise.

"Once *too* often," he replied. "I will know better another time."

"On what matter—" I began, but he said sharply, "'Tis none of your affair."

Everyone who came into the shop that day spoke of the comet, and Father soon forgot he'd doubted me, and began to brag instead that I'd seen it. I pretended not to hear him, but smiled to myself as I helped as usual at the counter. It was a good day. The shop windows faced east into Little Britain Street, and the day was fine; the dust motes circled in the morning light and gave me a feeling of well-being. My father, too, regained his good spirits and was more like himself. He was brightly dressed in blue trousers and yellow waistcoat, and wore a wig of black curls not unlike the King's. He smiled broadly at everyone who came in, and remembered their names, and asked after their ailing mothers, and when he spoke of the comet he winked at me.

There was plenty of trade. Old Mr. Grove who lived next door came in for a copy of Foxe's *Book of Martyrs*. He was grave and alarmed, and said he prayed he would not live to see the calamity that was coming. A gallant came in with a laughing young lady on his arm: they wanted to buy Mr. Dryden's *Secret Love*. They spoke eagerly of the comet and what it might portend, as though their lives were dull and needed a flood or plague to liven them up. Then came Paul Winter, with the same tear in his scarlet waistcoat as yesterday and the day before. He could not afford to buy a book, much less pay to have it bound, but he paid us something so that he might read a book a little at a time while standing in the shop.

"Hullo, Meg," he said to me as I handed him the loose pages of *Paradise Lost*. He had been reading it for over a month now. "I suppose you slept through the heavenly commotion last night."

"Not a bit," I answered.

"What! Up past midnight! I was in bed myself."

"Pity upon you, sir, for leading such a dull life," I answered him, and he laughed.

"But truly, did you see it?" he asked.

"Truly, I saw it. I knew what it was, too."

"Did you! You're an uncommon girl. Pray, what did it look like?"

He was not teasing now, but his face was earnest and excited, and I felt flattered, as though the attention were for me. I described the comet as best I could, and when I was done he pointed his roll of pages at me and said, "You do not know your luck."

Then he took his book over to the window by the street, where the light fell upon the closely printed sheets.

I thought about what he said and knew he was wrong. I *did* know my luck, and rejoiced in it. Not because I had seen the comet—I was glad enough to have seen it, for it made good conversation, but nothing more than that. Better luck was to be the sole child of a man with the freedom of the Stationers' Company, which regulated all the publishing, printing, bookselling, and bookbinding in London. Better luck was to be heir to such a man, to his volumes and his copyrights—and his china plates, for that matter. I would not live my life like other women, bound to dreary husbands and household duties. Instead, I would marry into the trade and be a bookseller like my father. I would be sought after by authors, would dine with great playwrights, and someday, at my father's side, I would drink my coffee with the Town wits at Will's Coffee House in Bow Street.

That was my plan.

❦ 4 ❧

T here were dozens of different almanacs, of course, but we sold only two, the two we published ourselves. One was *News from the Stars*, done by Andrews. The other was Barker's, and one afternoon, when the shop grew quiet, I took up this almanac and began to study it, thinking to find a clue to my father's strange ways. My father himself had gone on an errand to the Stationers' Company, leaving his chief apprentice, Robert, in charge of the shop, with me to help. Robert was twenty. He was short and moonfaced, with an eye that wandered. He was earnest and worked hard and did not run off to play football with the other apprentices. He never forgot the instructions my father gave him, and he recorded in my father's ledgers every farthing got or spent. But he read only for duty, not for pleasure, and he never ventured an idea about what sort of book might sell well. My father said he had no imagination and would never be a bookseller.

The day was cloudy and chill, and we kept the coal fire burning as we worked. There was no trade, so Robert took a rag and wiped the soot from the counters and boxes and stacks of books. He would rather do that than read. As for me, I settled myself on a stool near the window with Barker's almanac and made myself acquainted with it.

There was a table of the moons, a tide table, a description of the highways in England and Wales, and a list of fairs. None of these was helpful. The prognostications, however, seemed more promising. "In the month of April, bad news will be received from across the sea, and there is a chance of loss," I read. I pondered this for some moments, thinking of my father's correspondence and who might write to him from France or Flanders. But nothing occurred to me. I read on: "Storms may occur in the late part of April." I did not care about storms. "A man of the nobility, or one who is eminent in the arts, will depart this world, or will labor under discomfort." This alarmed me for a moment, but at last I decided that my father was not "eminent in the arts," being at bottom a merchant.

I scanned through the months. Sun in Aries, transit of Mars through Gemini, conjunction of Saturn and Mars . . . religious controversies anticipated . . . a martial undertaking . . . discord between nations . . . many people will be choleric and ill-tempered this month. That, indeed, might apply to my father. Nothing else was of use. I put the almanac carefully in its place—it sold for three pence, after all—and decided that the only reasonable course before me was to consult Anthony Barker, astrologer, himself.

Mr. Barker was my father's age, a friendly, untidy man who answered the most casual questions with a thoughtful air. It was three weeks before I could meet with him, for my time was not my own. May Day passed, and the milk-maids and sweeps paraded through the streets, and others went into the fields to gather the May dew. But I did not. I was busy thinking how I would pay Mr. Barker, for I had none but household money to spend. Fortune was with me, however, for a few days later I was sent to buy a length of muslin. I made such a good bargain that there was something to spare, and I looked on it as mine. And so at last I was able to send the boy Godfrey with a note for Mr. Barker explaining my need, and to meet him at his home near St. Clement's one morning while my father thought I was out buying Bristol soap.

I liked going out into the smoky, noisy streets of London. Overhead the carved and painted shop signs swung and banged in the wind, and apprentices yelled at all who passed to enter their masters' shops and buy there. A tinker beat upon a brass kettle with a stick, crying, "Have you a frying pan to mend?" A peddler hollered, "Flounders! Who'll buy my flounders?" and I smelled the strong stink of raw fish. Another peddler cried that he had lily-white vinegar to sell. I kept my step quick and my eyes upturned, that I might not have garbage or slops thrown onto me from the windows above as I walked.

The din grew worse as a coach came by; its wheels rattled on the cobblestones. I looked up at it and saw an

African in the box. He was dressed in fine livery but was barefoot and wore an iron collar around his neck; I knew it had engraved upon it the name of the nobleman who was his owner. I wondered whether the comet had blazed in the land where he was born, and whether his people knew how to read the stars.

Mr. Barker's home was fine though not grand. It was in the new Dutch style, all brick and pillars, and stood near the Flying Horse inn. The maidservant let me in, and led me to the small parlor, where Mr. Barker sat before a grate of burning coals. I hoped I would see Mr. Barker's collection, for he was famous for gathering rocks and bones and beetles. But the parlor was much like our own, with white walls hung with looking glasses, and a red piece of turkey work upon a table.

I told him what I wanted, but at first he did not take me seriously. "You are too young to need my services," he said, smiling. "I guess that your question is matrimonial, and my advice is simple. Leave all that to your father."

"Indeed, sir, marriage is not on my mind," I answered him. "I seek instead to know how the stars influence my father."

At this he lost his smile, and told me roughly to be gone, or he would tell my father.

"Stay, Mr. Barker. Why is not my need as great as any who come to you for help? Is any fate so uncertain as a child's? I am only looking for a signpost, that I may know how best to ride the currents of my fortune." This last was rather cleverly said, if I may say so, for it was exactly what he wrote at the start of his almanac.

He looked at me a moment as though trying not to laugh, and at last he smiled. "I cannot cast your father's nativity for you," he said. " 'Twould be improper. But I will tell you a little of your own fate, if you like."

"It is my own fate which interests me most of all," I said.

Mr. Barker asked me about my birth, its time and place, and after that he sat scratching his quill on his paper and looking at the charts in the very almanac I'd consulted myself three weeks before. I sat primly on a fine cane chair. The looking glass opposite me showed a bit of the room beyond, through the doorway, and I stretched my neck to see if I could spy his collection, but I could not.

At last Mr. Barker finished and laid his quill in a tray of sand. He folded his great, inky hands together and looked at me so soberly I grew afraid, but I said nothing.

"A great change is coming to your life," he said.

"For good or for ill?"

"That will depend upon you. You will be as a boat on the sea, tossed by powers beyond your control. Still, you are the pilot of that boat, and everything will depend upon the course you steer. Remember always to head *into* the wind, and do not flee it. Otherwise, you may capsize your boat."

"But what sort of a change?"

His voice was gentle. "You will suffer a great loss."

"Not—not my father!"

"I am speaking of your own life, child, not your father's."

This only bewildered me, and I tried to ask more questions, such as when this loss would befall me. But he would not say more, and instead began to shoo me from his rooms. As the maidservant took me to the door he called after me, "Remember, you are the pilot!" But I thought it poor consolation when he had given me such a dreadful fright—and at my own expense, too.

❦ 5 ❧

It was on Sunday next that I learned what my great loss was to be. I saw it for myself that morning, and was told straight out that evening after supper.

Hester saw it, too, but did not know she was seeing it.

We had gone again to St. Botolph's Bishopsgate. I did not care for Reverend Little, but I liked the walk, for it took us all through the City. The morning was gray, and the air from the Thames River floated damp against our cheeks, but I did not care. Hester and I walked in front with my father, and behind us came Cook and Jane, the serving girl, then Robert with Charles and James, the other apprentices. Godfrey, the boy, walked sometimes next to Jane, and sometimes with the older boys, that he might hear their chatter. We passed by the stones and beams they were putting together at St. Paul's, to rebuild the cathedral,

and I pointed with great excitement to a fine column. My
father only shook his head and said he did not think that it
would ever be done. We walked through Cheapside, and
saw the ruins of churches burnt in the Great Fire that de-
stroyed so much of London my second year of life. But
in the same street we saw the new shops of goldsmiths,
drapers, and haberdashers. The shops were shut up for the
Sabbath, of course, but the streets were filled with people
in their Sunday finery, nodding and bowing to one another. They were filled, too, with ne'er-do-wells who were
playing when they ought to have been at church. We saw
some young apprentices sitting on steps and waving their
tankards at one another while they told jokes. One of
them called out to our boys to join them; Charles said he
would, and Robert cuffed him. We walked on through
Threadneedle Street. I heard a shrill crow of pain, and
looking down a narrow lane I caught a glimpse of a cock-
fight.

I do not know which I loved more, seeing the folk who
bowed and nodded and worried about the weather, or seeing the boys who would certainly be fined for staying away
from divine service if they were caught. Both were a part
of life in London, and that I loved most of all.

Hester, however, loved it not. "Look at this," she would
say as she stepped over the turds someone had emptied
from a chamber pot into the street. "What a filthy place
London is."

And so it was, and so it is, but I have never minded it.

St. Botolph's was dark and old, for it was not burnt in

the Great Fire. I sat with my cloak pulled close amid the dreary, chill, stone monuments, and paid little attention to song and prayer. But I listened more carefully to the preaching, as was my habit, for sometimes a good sermon can be published with profit. However, the Reverend Little's words would find no wider audience; he made dull what should have stirred us all.

When the service was done, Hester and I stood in the lane outside and curtsied to this merchant and that neighbor. The draper and his wife bade me good morning with wide smiles, and their grown daughter, Susannah, spoke to me by name, which surprised me. "I have seen you in your father's shop," she said. She smiled as she said it, but I felt accused, as though she had said I should not be there.

"And I have seen you there," I answered her. All the grown folk laughed, and began to chat among themselves, while I waited impatiently to move on. But we did not move on, and at last Hester and I drew off, and murmured to one another as we listened to my father pay extravagant compliments to the draper's daughter.

"Beauty!" I repeated to Hester, having heard the word escape my father's mouth. "If bread is beautiful, then so is Susannah Beckwith."

"Or if coal is beautiful," Hester said.

"If lard is beautiful."

"If sand is beautiful."

"Sand *is* beautiful," I answered.

"Well, so is Susannah Beckwith's gown, even if her face is plain. Look at it."

I looked. And I looked some more. She was wearing a blue velvet gown drawn back to show a yellow underskirt, and the ruffles of her embroidered chemise showed at her neck. Her yellow hood was cast back to show off her hair, which was wired in ringlets that hung at the sides of her face. "Now, why is *she* all dressed up?" I said as I watched her simper at my father, but as soon as I spoke I knew the answer. I knew why we'd been going to St. Botolph's, and why my father was not himself, and where he'd been when he ought to have been dining with John Dryden. I knew what my great loss was going to be—my very inheritance. The only thing I didn't know was how to head into the wind.

I didn't say anything to Hester. My tongue felt like a brick in my mouth. I knew there was no use lashing out, no use crying or ranting. What I needed was caution, and a plan.

"Catching herself a husband, I suppose," Hester said, answering my question.

I did not speak, but my head felt hot from the fury of my thinking.

He did not look at me when he told me. He looked at his pipe, stuffing it and prodding it as he readied himself for a smoke. We sat together in the small parlor, Hester being busy with her duties.

"I have news," he said.

"Good news, I hope," I said, to torment him.

"Good news indeed," he replied, but he knew I would not think so. "I have decided to marry again."

"Father! My greatest congratulations. I have long awaited such news. Your betrothed must count herself lucky indeed to marry so fine a man."

My father looked surprised and much relieved.

"Thank you, Margaret," he said. "I believe she does so. I am to marry Susannah Beckwith at the end of June. The banns will be read next week."

"Susannah Beckwith?" I repeated. I spoke as though I could not believe my ears. "Have you not heard—but it is not my place—Susannah Beckwith. Oh. I wish you both joy, of course. Susannah Beckwith."

He did not ask me what I meant, but I could see by the dismay in his face that he believed me. Why should he not? He had known me long, and knew it was not my custom to pretend what I did not feel. Neither is it my custom, however, to be cheated of what is mine.

THE LADIES' CALLING

My father often dined away from home, but from time to time he invited others to dine with him instead. When company came, I used always to eat with Hester in the small parlor, whilst the apprentices and servants ate in the kitchen. But over the past year, my father had asked me more and more often to dine with him, and if I kept silence well through the first course, he sometimes invited me to speak during the second. I loved these occasions, for it is a fine thing to listen to wit and raillery, or even to argument, though keeping silence is not so easy.

I did not find it easy on the Sunday that Mr. Pennyman and his wife came to dine after church.

Everything was laid out most elegantly for the Pennymans. Jane had brought two chairs from the parlor, making four altogether. The napkins were of fine linen, the plates of china, and there were forks as well as spoons and knives. There was even one for me. It was a sunny day, and the afternoon light fell soft upon the wooden floor-boards, while the kitchen smells floated pleasantly into the room.

Cook had done her best to keep our tongues enter-tained with the dinner, for the bill of fare included stewed carp, a boiled pudding, a chine of veal, a calf's head pie, a roasted chicken, and a salad made with the buds of herbs and violets. The stewed carp was not well seasoned, but the calf's head pie had a tasty crust, and the chicken was golden and juicy. However, the food could not keep me happy. It was that morning that the banns had been read for the first time, and the Pennymans were full of congratulations for my father, which sounded harsh in my ears.

My father and I had spoken no more about his wed-ding. After I planted in his head the idea that there might be scandal to be discovered about Susannah Beckwith, I hoped that he might delay the wedding while he made his investigations. But it is one thing to plant an idea, and an-other to make it grow. Still, the banns were to be read for two more weeks before the wedding could take place, and anything might happen in that time. I was most hopeful that my father's intended bride had already been married, secretly and imprudently, and that her husband was yet liv-ing and would come forward to forbid the banns. I had heard of such things happening before, and it seemed to me both possible and proper that such a thing might happen now. The almanac foretold bad news from across the sea, and a husband in Flanders would be bad news indeed for Susannah Beckwith. However, I did not mean to leave everything to the stars.

At the start of the dinner my elders discoursed on political matters. They spoke of the Earl of Shaftesbury and his friends, and how the King would handle him, and what ought to be done about the Papists. Then they spoke on more general topics, such as the weather, and the affairs of mutual friends, and the comet. And at last they spoke of the printed word, which in our household always became the subject of discussion sooner or later.

Mr. Pennyman was the author of *A Wife's Misdeeds*, which we had published last Hilary term. It was about how immoral women are, and how closely they must be watched by their husbands to prevent them from taking their marital pleasures elsewhere. It pretended to be the tale of a young and lustful wife named Miranda, but there was very little tale, and much dreary lecturing. However, we sold many copies, for infidelity is always an interesting subject.

"I believe my daughter has read your work," my father said to Mr. Pennyman as the roasted chicken was brought in. "Margaret?"

He often gave me a chance of this sort. I was expected to flatter the authors sweetly, and not to advance my own views, though a few times I asked mischievious questions out of pretended innocence. My father always scolded me afterward, but in a way that showed he was well pleased, for he valued my wit in spite of himself.

"Indeed," I said. "I found it both clever and instructive. It is finding a large audience, as well it should." Mr. Pennyman smiled largely, and his wife gave a firm nod. "I wonder, sir, if you might answer a question for me," I continued.

"Certainly," he said, but his wife frowned faintly, as though she thought I was impertinent.

"Miranda's conduct was a disgrace to our sex, it is true. But ought not her husband to have expected such troubles when they married? For she was younger than he, and did not marry for love."

"Certainly not!" said Mrs. Pennyman. I knew before I spoke that what I said would not be agreeable to her, for she was far younger than her husband. But it mattered more to me that Susannah Beckwith was only a girl compared with my father. "What sort of education have you had, girl, to ask such a question? Chastity does not derive from love, but from obedience to God's law."

"Because she was young, it does not follow that she did not love," my father said as though he could not help himself.

"But how can a man of means, himself no longer young, ever know that a young woman chooses him for love and not for money?" I asked, as though I wanted only to learn.

"A man of more years is also a man of greater wis-

dom," Mr. Pennyman said. "And a better judge of charac-
ter." Then he looked to my father, as though to ask why he
did not put a stop to my pertness.

"Enough, Margaret," my father said. "You speak of
what you do not yet understand." He spoke almost in a
mumble, but when I looked at his face I saw it was white,
and I knew there would be more to come when the guests
had gone.

I thought he would call me to the small parlor, where
he often worked, but instead he found me with Hester,
bundling the laundry, and bade me follow him. I did so,
and he led me to the kitchen. Cook was not there, though
a great kettle hung over the fire.

"I have never heard such rudeness, Margaret," he said,
and his voice was unlike itself, filled with uneasy anger. "I
never thought to hear such rudeness from *you*. I know
your education has been irregular. But by God you know
more than to disgrace me in that way. I must beat you for
it." And he picked up the broom.

I opened my mouth to speak—it was my habit, always,
to speak—but said nothing. I had been beaten a few times
as a child, of course, when I was six or seven. My mother
beat me, that I might learn obedience. But not since her
death had I had bruises at a parent's hand. And all that
came into my head now was that it must not happen.

"Well? Speak, Daughter!"

Perhaps he meant that I should talk my way out of it, as

I talked him round on so many things. I wanted to. But I could not find the words, could not speak. I only looked at the bundle of sticks and straw he held in his hand and thought: He will not do it. He cannot do it.

But he did. He lifted the broom and swung it at me and it caught me on the shoulder. My body was as surprised as if my brain had given it no notice, and I fell. He struck again, and I felt the sting of straw on my arm. Then he dropped the broom and walked away.

The stones of the floor felt cold, though I was so near the fire. They felt so cold. I did not want to cry, lying there alone in the great kitchen. But I cried anyway.

✳ **2** ✳

I stayed in my chamber all that day. The room I shared with Hester was small and dark, with no window and no cabinet, only a chest for our clothing and a row of pegs along the wall. But there was a night table on either side of the big wooden bed, each littered with candle stubs and mine piled high with pages.

I did not come down for supper that night. I said I was not hungry, but Hester brought me apples and bread and butter and part of a quince cake left over from dinner, and I ate it all. I ate as though apples were my enemies, for I was very angry and did not mean to be defeated.

"What roused him so?" Hester asked, while she rubbed ointment onto the red welt on my arm. She had made the ointment herself, in the stillroom. I sat on our bed while she knelt before me, and watched the candlelight move in the dark, silky hair that was pinned behind her neck. Her face was truly pretty, and her teeth fine and white, but the hands she used to soothe my burning skin were large and red and rough.

"Susannah Beckwith rouses him," I answered her.

"But what did you say, Meg, that angered him?"

"Nothing. Only I asked Mr. Pennyman if a man of means who married a woman much younger than he might not expect that she had married him for money instead of love."

"Oh, Meg!" She stopped rubbing and sat back on her heels. "For shame."

"It was only a question. Only words. Can there be shame in words?"

"You know there can be, and most of all in a woman's mouth."

"I am not a woman yet."

"And ought not to be allowed at table, in consequence. I suppose you will be allowed no more." She rose to her feet and began wiping her hands on her apron.

What she said was very likely to be true, and made me want to cry again. To keep the tears back I said stubbornly, "If there is any shame it belongs to those who do the deed, not to those who speak of it."

Hester shook her head. "There is no shame in a widower marrying again, Meg."

"Not her. Not Susannah Beckwith. There is something very wrong with her, I know."

"That's foolish talk. You know nothing of her."

"You're wrong. I've heard—I *know* there is something very ill in her, something that would keep my father from marrying if he but knew." In truth I had heard nothing of the girl, but I was so sure I was right it did not matter to me that I bent the truth a little.

"Why, what have you heard?"

"Nothing to prove, so we must find out the rest. You know the kitchenmaid at the Beckwiths, do you not? Perhaps she has heard secrets that can help us. You must go to her—"

"Stop it! Stop it!"

Hester took my shoulders and gave me a shake. "You must stop this, Meg! You will bring yourself to ruin! Pity your poor father, who has been so good to you all these years and taught you his trade and shared his gossip and had you at table to meet famous men. Is this the gratitude you give him, at a time that should be all joy for him? Margaret, Margaret, you forget yourself."

And then I knew that I was indeed alone, abandoned by friend as well as father, scorned by all because I would not do a daughter's duty.

"I'm tired," I said. "I will go to bed early tonight."

Hester was silent a long moment. "Pray well," she said at last. "And I will pray, too, that God and your father will forgive you." She reached to the row of pegs that lined the wall and handed me my nightdress.

The next morning I went to my father and said, "I beg your pardon, Father, that I forgot myself at table yesterday and said things that so displeased you."

He looked at me as though bewildered and said, "I could not believe it when you spoke so."

So I knew that he had not forgiven me. I saw myself through his eyes, and I began to feel shame.

Trade was slow in the shop that day. On some slow days I was sent with Robert to open a stall at St. Paul's Churchyard, and vie with the other booksellers there for the buyers who passed. I hoped it would be so today, that I might be away from my father, but it seemed he could not bring himself even to speak to me, so instead I sat on a three-legged stool near the window and read, and he turned his pages behind the counter.

I read *The Ladies' Calling*, by Richard Allestree. I had not cared to read it before, though I had heard it much admired. But that morning I was filled with fear that I had driven from me all who once loved me, and I read with the hope of redeeming myself.

This is what I learned from Richard Allestree:

Nothing is more important than modesty. Modesty appears in the face in calm and meek looks. Nothing gives a greater luster to feminine beauty. If there is boldness in a woman's face, it blots out all the lines of beauty, like a cloud over the sun.

A modest woman does not show earnestness or loud-
ness in discourse. A woman's tongue should be like the
imaginary music of the spheres, sweet and charming, but
not to be heard at a distance.

Talkativeness is a fault to be found in none but the
bold. There can be no greater indecency in conversation
than that a woman should monopolize it.

All that I learned threw me into despair. I understood
better now how very ill I had behaved, and what a coarse,
bold girl I was, and how I must disgust all who knew and
met me, most especially my father and Hester. But it did
not seem likely to me that I could amend my ways, for
they were very set indeed. I could not keep my tongue
from galloping, for it merely raced to the command of the
thoughts and feelings which rode upon it. I could not keep
meekness in my face, for I felt it not, and had not suffi-
cient discipline of mind to keep a lie upon my features for
more than a few seconds at a time.

My face must have been honest indeed when Paul Winter walked into the shop. "Come," he said. "It can't be as
bad as that."

I looked across at my father, but he was examining the
pages of a book on navigation and mathematics newly
sent from the printer, and paid no heed. "Good morning,
Mr. Winter," I said as brightly as I could. "Are you here for
Paradise Lost?"

"Nay, I finished it at last. What a wondrous book it is!
Have you read it?"

"A little, only. I am more fond of plays than poetry, especially Puritan poetry." As soon as I spoke I remembered that it would not do to give my views so freely. Now Mr. Winter, too, would think me bold and coarse and no proper daughter to my father. "I beg your pardon, sir," I said, looking down at the pages of Mr. Allestree's book.

He looked surprised, but did not ask me what I meant. Instead he said, "I am looking for something new to read. Can you recommend something?"

"There is Mr. Wycherley's play, *The Plain-Dealer*—it is selling very well."

"I saw it when it was at the Duke's Theatre."

"There is a new book of dialogues from Thomas Hobbes of Malmesbury."

"That is more like. I am in the mood for philosophy. What is it you read yourself?"

I was nearly embarrassed to tell him, as though he would know at once why I read it. "*The Ladies' Calling*, sir."

"Ah, I have heard much of it. Do you find it advises you well?"

"Very well, sir. But I fear I have much to change in myself before I can acquire the virtues Mr. Allestree commends."

Mr. Winter smiled so broadly that I felt affronted, though I hardly knew why. He saw it in my too-honest face and made his own face grave. "And what virtues does Mr. Allestree commend that you lack?" he asked.

"I am too talkative, sir."

He could not keep himself from smiling again, but this

time I smiled, too. Mr. Winter glanced over at my father, but a gentleman had come in and they were much engaged in discussion. "Did you know that not everyone agrees with Mr. Allestree in his ideas?" Mr. Winter asked. "Margaret Fell believes women can be preachers, and has written an essay to say so."

"Margaret Fell is a Quaker," I said.

"At the sign of the Three Balls they sell a pamphlet by Bathsua Makin in which she argues that women should be taught Latin and Greek. And I have read a book of poems by Katherine Philips. Have you heard of her?"

"I have . . . but we do not sell her work, so I have not read it."

"Many women are speaking their minds in these times. I hesitate to mention Aphra Behn . . . "

This time we both looked at my father, who was just bidding the gentleman goodbye. He had not heard us. Aphra Behn was a woman playwright, the only one in the history of the world, as far as I knew. There were many scandalous rumors about her and she was known to have low companions. Mr. Allestree certainly would not have allowed her near his wife and daughters.

"Going to buy something today, Mr. Winter?" my father asked, as though he thought Mr. Winter had been standing about too long without money changing hands.

"I only wish I had the means," Mr. Winter replied, taking a coin from his waistcoat pocket. "But if I might have a look at Hobbes's new dialogues here in the shop . . ."

"Of course, of course," my father said, and took the money with one hand, while with the other he reached for the book where it lay unbound on the counter.

❧ 3 ❧

T he banns were read for the second time on the next Sunday, and for the last time the Sunday following. I waited hopefully, but was twice more disappointed. If Susannah Beckwith had indeed been secretly married, her husband was keeping himself busy elsewhere.

"She has sent him to the country to hunt for deer, for she means to have venison at the wedding feast," I said to Hester.

"Nay, he has gone to Spain to buy silks for her gown," Hester answered.

"To Portugal for brandy, that she might be drunk on her wedding night."

"To Bristol for soap, that she might be clean!"

"To the wise woman in his village, for a cordial to make my father strong enough to withstand his bride when she comes to the bridal bed."

"Meg, you go too far," Hester said.

I did not mind her reproof. It was enough that she was bantering with me once more, as we used to do. She did not truly mind what I said of Susannah Beckwith behind my father's back, so long as I did not offend his ear or try to stop his happiness. As for my father, he, too, had forgiven me, and was only too glad to be smiling and nodding until the curls of his wig bobbed, and pretending things were the same as they ever were. But of course they were not, and we all knew it.

During those days I was most careful of my conduct in my father's presence. I spoke courteously, did not interrupt, did not ask impertinent questions, did not forward my views. Mr. Allestree would have been proud of me. By the day before the wedding I thought I would die of meekness.

There were few customers, and the day was fine, and I was angry at my father for marrying and equally because he made me stay within doors when the sun was shining. He was nervous himself, and made the apprentices come running when he needed them not, and fretted because he believed he had lost things that were there before his face. At last he looked at me without pleasure and said sharply, "Go, leave."

"Where ought I to go?" I asked, thinking he meant to send me on an errand.

"Anywhere you like," he said, and fished a shilling from his pocket.

I could not believe my good fortune. I had never before in my life had an afternoon of freedom with all of London to enjoy and a shilling with which to enjoy it. I ran from the shop, and nearly bumped into our neighbor Mr. Turner, who was passing our door at the moment. Mr. Turner lived with his father and his brother and his two grown sons—five Mr. Turners in one house and not a woman among them, except for the servants.

"Margaret, Margaret, do not be so hasty!" he chided me, catching me by the shoulder that I might not collide with him. "Where do you go in such a hurry?"

"I do not know, sir," I answered him, and indeed, I did not. This was London Town, full of noise and riches and marvels, and there were a thousand things I might do.

I could watch the Punch and Judy, or listen to ballad-singers on the street corners. I could pay tuppence at Charing Cross to see a dead calf that had been born with two heads; Godfrey had seen the crowds around it the day before while carrying a message to the printer. I could fol-low a great coach through the town and watch the lords and ladies alight at journey's end. I might even see the King.

Or I might seek out a play by Aphra Behn.

The idea was sudden and bold. I stood staring at Mr. Turner's broad back in its dark velvet jacket as he made his way down Little Britain, and when I could see him no longer I looked cautiously about. I was not sure who sold her plays. There might be a copy right in this street, where so many booksellers had their shops. But I did not want my father to see me inquiring of our neighbors. Instead, I made my way to St. Paul's Churchyard, where the book-sellers kept their stalls.

It was not far to walk, but I walked slowly, as though this were my last chance ever to enjoy London. I peered into every dim shop to eye the wares: bright cloth or copper pots or newly printed pages. I paused near the turnip peddler's cart, and turned over his roots as though I meant to buy. I drew a deep breath by the door of a cookshop, and smelled the spicy meat pasties baking within. I spent not a farthing, but by the time I reached the bookstalls I was nearly sated with the pleasure of things I had not bought.

I was well known among the booksellers at St. Paul's, but it took me long to find what I sought, for I was at first too shy to ask for it. Instead I lingered at first one stall and then another, chattering idly with the booksellers about pamphlets and broadsides newly printed. At length I would drive the conversation toward the publication of plays, and the names would come drifting down like snow: Dryden and Wycherley, Etherege and Otway. I had been over an hour at the bookstalls when Mr. Fletcher said: "And of course, we publish Mrs. Behn, but you are not interested in her."

"My father spoke of her last week, and was wanting to read one of her plays, as a curiosity. Perhaps I may surprise him with it."

In the end I took it away with me, and found a green place to sit in Lincoln's Inn Fields, in sight of the fashionable brick houses there. The play was called *The Rover*, and had been an amazing success at Dorset Gardens a month or so ago. I settled down to read it, and the afternoon wore on without my noticing, for it was a remarkable play. It was remarkable because it was so little different from a play writ by a man: it was as funny, as bawdy, as silly. And yet the fact that it was *not* by a man seemed to echo on every page, and filled me with wonder and anger and a secret sense of intention. For if a woman might think so like a man, and write so like a man . . . then why might not a woman give her views at table without apology?

⇾ 4 ⇽

"D id you see the wedding ring?" I asked Hester the next morning, while we were still abed. "It's covered in jewels."

Hester shook her head. Her long hair danced on the pillow. "Wedding rings smack of popery, to my mind."

"Oh, Hester, you're nearly a Puritan. I suppose you have refused the new dress my father bought you for the wedding?"

Hester smiled broadly, and a great dimple showed in her face. For all her bantering with me, she smiled but seldom. When she did, it made me feel happy, though I had promised myself to be nothing but surly on this, my father's wedding day.

"Nay, I'm grateful enough for a new gown," Hester said. "And so are you, I vow."

I was. My dress was red velvet with three-quarter sleeves, and the sleeves of the chemise I wore beneath fell in lovely white pleats. There were satin bows all over my clothing—on my shoulders and bodice and skirt. Even my shoes were new.

It was early yet when people began to gather at the house, all dressed in their finest silks and velvets. They laughed and drank and made coarse jokes and laughed some more. Though I had been determined not to be merry, before long I was merry in spite of myself, for I was teased and twirled and given gloves and ribbons and bride-knots to wear, and I could not help liking it.

Everyone was there. Neighbors like Mr. Grove and the five Mr. Turners. Authors like Mr. Coles and Mr. Andrews. Mr. Pennyman came with his wife. They were given ribbons to wear, and Mrs. Pennyman got exceedingly drunk. Mr. Barker was there. He clapped my father on the back, and said the best astrologers could make mistakes. Other booksellers came, including Mr. Fletcher, who had sold me Aphra Behn's play. I prayed he would not ask my father how he liked it. Even some of our favored customers came, such as old Mr. Bledsoe, who worked for the Navy. Paul Winter was there, too, though no one had invited him.

The Beckwith family was there, of course, and many friends with them, mostly other merchants in the City. Mr. Allington was a goldsmith, and Mr. Gosse was a vintner. Mr. Gosse brought his entire family, and they were many, both older and younger than I. There was a laughing girl who spent her whole time looking after the younger children, including a baby. I could not see what she had to laugh at. Her face was pitted from the smallpox and her dress was not as nice as mine. But then, everyone was laughing that day.

We all went to the church together, laughing our way through the streets, while a fiddler and a drummer led the way. There was so much merriment, indeed, that it was hard to grow sober for the ceremony. I sat near to old Mr. Bledsoe, who wanted to tickle me throughout, which I did not want. So I changed places with Hester, who frowned at him until he became sulky. By then the sermon on matrimony was nearly over.

And then came my last chance, for Reverend Little said solemnly: "If any man can show any just cause why they may not lawfully be joined together, let him now speak, or else hereafter forever hold his peace."

I clasped my gloved hands together tightly and prayed to hear a voice ring out, but there was only giggling and snoring. So Reverend Little spoke on, and asked my father if he would take Susannah Beckwith to be his wife, "forsaking all other," and my father said he would. Then came the ring, which my father put on the fourth finger of her left hand, for there is a vein there that runs straight to the heart, they say. And at last he said: "With this ring I thee wed, with my body I thee worship, and with all my worldly goods I thee endow."

Those worldly goods were supposed to be mine.

Then we all went home again. Someone broke a cake over Susannah's head when she went through the door, as is the custom, but I wished it were a brick instead.

Next came the feast. The wedding dinner had been ordered from a cookshop, and was carried through the streets in a grand procession to our house. On the table were platters of asparagus, buttered shrimps, roast pigeon, a side of lamb, a lamprey pie, a turkey stuffed with cloves, grapes boiled in butter and served with bread and sugar, three kinds of tart, and ever so much more. I think I never saw so much food before, nor ate so much. The merrier my father grew, the more I put into my mouth, as if to keep my angry tongue from trouble. At last I felt full to bursting, and climbed behind the sideboard in the large parlor, where I leaned against the leather wall-hanging and sat with my eyes closed and my hand on my belly. It was well I did for soon they all began to play kissing games. Everyone laughed and clapped when my father took his bride in his arms and kissed her lustfully, and then others began to do the like. I heard Mr. Bledsoe saying, "Where's the little one? Where's the girl?" and I was glad I had hid myself. A bit later I heard Hester saying, "La, what are you thinking of?" I peeped out, and saw Mr. Fletcher kissing her and pulling at her laces, so I ducked down again.

At last I dozed, even amid so much noise. I dreamed that my mother was looking for me, saying in a voice filled with yearning, "Where is my daughter? Where is my daughter?" I tried to answer her but I could not, for my tongue had a bride-ribbon tied around it. It had been put there so that I might stay a modest girl and not talk too freely. I woke to a great shout and cries of "The posset! The posset!"

Then I came out, and saw my father and his bride given the posset to drink, which was made of wine, milk, egg-yolks, cinnamon, sugar, and nutmeg. It was supposed to fortify them for the night to come. Then we all trooped upstairs. A brideman pulled off Susannah's garters and fastened them to his hat. My father's men took him aside to undress him, and the bridesmaids did the same for her, until both were put to bed in their night things. Then the bridemen sat at the foot of the bed and threw her stockings over their shoulders toward the bride, retrieving them and trying again until one at last hit her right in the nose. There was much laughter, and it was said that brideman would be next to marry. And the bridesmaids threw my father's stockings at him, and the same was said of the one who hit him. At last we left them alone in bed, and went downstairs where we continued to make merry far into the night. At least, some of us did, but Hester and I went to our room not so very much later. She went right to sleep, in spite of the noise. But I lay long awake, and tried not to listen at all.

THE QUEEN-LIKE CLOSET

1

Where is my daughter?" said a voice, but it was not my mother's voice. It was the voice of Susannah Beckwith, who was now Susannah Moore.

I did not answer, but she found me anyway in the small parlor, where I was reading a manuscript my father had left on the little table there. My father spent much of his time in this room, and it was always in great disorder. Papers were piled everywhere, and there he kept his pens, and inkpots, and the tray of sand he used to blot his words when they were written. A great clutter of objects lay about: a paper knife, an empty tankard, several of my father's pipes. Dust lay upon everything, for Jane and Hester were forbidden to come in with their rags. My father did not like things disturbed.

There were two chairs there. My father by custom sat

always in one, and I in the other. Mine was cane. My father's had an embroidered cushion with small blue flowers, done by my mother years ago. Now it was grimy with soot, and worn away in places from my father's sitting. Sometimes, when he was not in the house, I sat upon his chair and read his papers. It was not my job to do so, but he never minded, and I was curious to read the things he would not publish as well as the things he would.

"Margaret," my stepmother said. I looked up at her, but for a moment she said no more. She looked around the untidy room and then cast her eyes heavenward. "Something must be done about this room!" she said, and smiled at me as though she thought I would agree.

"Father likes it this way," I answered.

Her smile faded. She regarded me with a grave and kindly air. At last she said, "You have been long without a mother, but that is past. You are my daughter now, and I am your mother."

"I do not need a mother," I said. "I have Hester."

"Hester has not taught you all that you must know."

I looked down at my page, but she put her hand across it, so that I found myself staring at the jeweled ring on her left hand instead of the close handwriting I had been squinting at the moment before.

"I have been discussing your education with your father. How he made me laugh! What a sorry wife you would make if you were to marry now. Fortunately, you need not think of that. We have time enough to teach you all you must learn. More time in the kitchen, that is what you need, and let the apprentices take care of the shop."

"I do not want to be taken from the shop."

"You need not fear, Margaret. I am not sending you to drudge in the kitchen. Hester, Jane, and Cook will do our bidding, and you will learn to make plague-waters and healing teas and to order a grand dinner and how to write out an invitation and what to say to the Lord Mayor, if he should come here. We will have great fun."

"The Lord Mayor has been here," I said.

She lifted her hand at last, and I bent my head to read again.

"Put that aside, Margaret."

I paid her no heed.

"Your father bade me take your education in hand, Meg. I am your mother now, and this is my household. Do you think I will fail of my duty to you?"

I looked up at her then, and saw that the kindness she began with had gone. There were spots of red in her pale cheeks, and her little eyes were nearly closed. I could see that she meant to have her way.

"Come with me, now," she said.

"Yes, Mother," I said. I stood swiftly and laid the sheaf of papers upon the table.

It surprised her, I saw, but she did not hesitate. She led the way to the stillroom. This was a small room near to the kitchen, where all manner of medicines were prepared for the household. The shelves were filled with dark bottles, some with stoppers and others covered with cloth. Bundles of herbs were pinned to the wall to dry, shedding their sharp scents into the air we inhaled. The room was not strange to me; I don't know how many times I had interrupted Hester there over the years. But as I stood there with my father's new wife it was not Hester I thought of, but my own mother. I remembered her there when Louis was dying, how she worked with grim face, and snapped at me when I tried to speak my fear. The memory was so strong and bitter I almost turned and ran. But I looked at my new mother and knew that hope did not lie in flight.

"Today I will teach you to make a powder which will help keep your teeth clean and sound. Hester says you do not use one now."

This was true. It was my custom to wipe my teeth with my linen napkin after dining, and nothing more. It was what my father had always done, and it seemed good enough to me.

"First we will take an ounce of white salt. See? Next, an ounce of cuttlebone. We will mix them together . . . "

Obediently I took the mortar and pestle and began to grind the cuttlebone.

That week we made tooth powder, a salve for the lips made of beeswax, a cordial of orange-water, and a remedy for children with rickets.

"I am the only child here," I said to her when she told me of this last, "and I do not have rickets."

My stepmother did not answer at once. She smiled and looked down at the counter, which she was cleaning with a rag. I knew she was thinking of the children she meant to bear to my father.

"A good closet has many remedies within," she said at last.

※ 2 ※

I was not made to leave the shop entirely, but it did not matter, for my pleasure there was spoilt. In the afternoons, when I yet helped behind the counter, *she* was there, too, welcoming those who came to buy and bossing the apprentices, while my father dined away from home and took himself to the Stationers' Hall or the printer's. Even Mr. Winter's visits were not the same. Now he gave his coin to Susannah instead of to me, and asked her about great men of the City, and what plays they most liked. In the mornings, when my father kept to the shop, I was kept from it, and I saw him but seldom now, except at table. I complained bitterly to Hester, but was wise enough to hold my tongue when my father was by, for he walked everywhere with his head lifted skyward and a great smile upon his face.

I did not understand him. She had turned our lives upside down. She had dusted and straightened the small parlor, and he did not even care. Now, if he sat there, she sat with him, on the cane chair that once was mine. But most often they sat together in the large parlor, which she filled with her pretty, silly things until I hardly knew it. I liked better to sit alone or with Hester in the small parlor, though it bore fewer and fewer traces of my father.

Not long after my lessons in housewifery began, I found a way to entertain myself at my stepmother's expense. We sold a book in the shop called *The Queen-like Closet*, by Hannah Woolley, which contained recipes of all kinds, for food and for medicines. It also included menus for fine dinners, and examples of proper letters written on diverse occasions. It was not a book that had interested me in the past, for I liked not to concern myself with women's business. But Hester had her own bound copy, which she often consulted. Now at last I, too, found it most valuable.

One evening, when my father was out and Hester busy with her duties, I sat with my stepmother in the large parlor and studied the book closely. "Mother," I said eagerly, "here is a recipe for a very sovereign water which will be of great use to you."

"Are you reading again, Meg? We must begin on your needlework soon, that you may be usefully occupied."

"You are reading yourself," I pointed out. She had before her a bound book with dark covers, though I could not say what it was, for I could not read the title from where I sat.

"I have mastered the arts you are still learning. Still, even I might be better occupied mending your father's torn waistcoat than wasting my time this way." And she gave a guilty glance to her book.

"I think you will find my time was not wasted tonight," I told her.

"What is it you have found, then? I do not think I need Mrs. Woolley's help in my kitchen or my stillroom."

"This very sovereign water is good for many ailments, but you will find it most especially useful as it helps speedily those with stinking breath."

She did not speak but her face filled up with red. I made my own face as innocent as I could. "Have I offended you? I thought I heard my father say—"

"Get out of here."

"I am waiting for my father."

"Get out. Go to your room. I do not want you before me."

"It also kills worms within the body. It helps with palsy. It is a cure for barrenness."

She stood, holding her book in her hand. Although twice my age, she was not greatly larger than myself, for I was a big girl and she a small woman. But I did not wish to be struck, so I rose myself. "I think I will find Hester," I said, and left the room, carrying *The Queen-like Closet* under my arm.

In the weeks that followed I was most obedient to my stepmother, attending to her carefully as she taught me to boil pigeons, to make Dr. Butler's treacle water, to make perfume of roses, to candy violets or gillyflowers. But when no one else was by I gave her many suggestions for remedies she needed not.

"Mrs. Woolley has an excellent surfeit-water which she says will help you with that farting."

"There is a fine remedy here which helps remove the pits of smallpox from your face—have you tried it?"

Each time I insulted her she sent me away, and each time I found Hester, and jested with her as we used to do.

When first I began these assaults upon Susannah I worried that she would bear tales to my father, and wondered how I would face him if his ire were roused. But soon I saw that she would not own to him that she could not manage me. And because she did not bear tales about me to my father, I thought that I was safe, and that I would remain so forever. However, I was wrong.

We had spent the morning in the kitchen, making a gooseberry fool to have for dessert that day. Susannah was in a fine humor; I believe she did not correct me once. When I spilled the rosewater she said it did not matter, and when she dropped a wooden plate she laughed at herself, and said she was not fit to be my teacher. Almost we had fun together. But I did not want to have fun with the one who was taking my inheritance from me.

And so, as we dusted ourselves clean, I said to her, "I see you have got the ink spots out of your linen apron."

Because we had laughed together, she was not on guard

against me, as she should have been. Instead, she looked surprised, and said, "There were no ink spots."

"Oh, I'm sorry. It was a natural mistake. Mrs. Woolley says ink spots on linen must be soaked in urine, so when I smelled you of course I thought . . . "

I had seen her angry with me before, but now she was not angry. Tears came to her eyes, and she turned from me.

"I must find Hester," I said, for I felt bad, and wanted to be away from the mischief I'd done.

"Hester," she repeated. "It is Hester who puts it into your head to say such things."

I was alarmed. "No, Mother, it is all my own thinking. I would not dare to speak so if Hester were near, do not beat her, please. Beat me, if you must."

But she went from the kitchen without looking at me again.

Then truly I ran to find Hester, to warn her. She scolded me when she heard what I had said, and hit at me, but I ducked back as she knew I would. Then we waited, but we heard nothing from my stepmother the rest of that day. In the shop she was cool to me, but she was often that.

The days passed. I learned to pickle cucumbers, and to preserve raspberries, and to make a trifle. I dared not make more sharp remarks to my mother, but I began to be very clumsy in the kitchen, spilling often, or measuring the wrong portions, or seeming stupid when she knew I was not.

Then, one evening after supper, my father called Hester to him, and when she came out of the parlor her face was white.

"What is it?" I cried, running to her, for I had been waiting on the stairs.

"I am dismissed," she said.

I gazed at her for one terrified moment, then flew into the parlor. My father was sitting in a chair, and Susannah stood before him. He held one of her hands in his, and smiled upon her.

"You must not, you must not," I said to him, and flung myself to my knees. Susannah stepped back in surprise. "Hester has done nothing. I am the one who makes the mischief from my own head; it is my fault! Do not send Hester away!"

"Meg, what is this nonsense? Calm yourself, Daughter." My father patted my hair soothingly. "Your mother needs a lady's maid, that is all; someone who can go with her to the theater and help her to dress her hair. She has found someone more fit for this service than Hester, that is all. Do not worry about Hester. She will have a handsome present before she goes back to her village."

I turned my face to look at my stepmother. Her eyes were as innocent as mine so often were with her. "Please," I said in a low voice. "I will not mock you. I will study your arts. I will not spill in the kitchen."

She smiled in a puzzled way at my father. "Do you think I am punishing you for a little spilled sugar, Margaret? Don't be foolish."

"I know you have been a good daughter to your new mother," my father said. "Susannah would have told me if it were otherwise. Do not bother yourself, Meg. Get up now. You need not come begging here."

I stood up.

"Read aloud to us a little, Meg. Susannah has not heard how beautifully you read."

"May I read another night, please? I have a headache."

"Of course, of course. Run along, then. Perhaps Hester may need you."

So once more I ran to Hester, and cried piteously, for I feared I had capsized my boat.

❧ 3 ❧

When once the shock was past, Hester did not mind so very much going home to her village. She had told me often that she did not love London, but I hardly believed her, for I loved it so much myself. And then, she was eager to see Thomas again, whom she would one day marry. "I hardly mind going, except for your sake, Meg," she said to me.

I did not tell her so, but this grieved me, and made me cry when she was not near to see. I wanted her to mind for her own sake, and not only for mine.

"It will not be so bad," she comforted me. "Perhaps your father will let you come to visit me in Surrey."

"That is likely enough, if I come soon, for he would like to be alone with his bride. Once she conceives, however, I will be needed here to wait on her hand and foot."

"Meg, it is not as bad as that."

But to me it was.

The first week of August brought four days in a row of hot weather. The meat pasties in the cookshops went bad in the heat, and the smells of the street grew fierce. It was on the fourth day that Hester left London. I rose very early, to breakfast with her before she went.

"Will Thomas meet the coach at Guildford?" I asked.

"He'll not be able to wait that long. He'll start in the night and walk ahead."

"He'll borrow the cooper's brown mare and ride the London road," I said.

"He'll turn himself into a bird and fly by the coach window."

"I wish *I* could turn myself into a bird."

"I do, too, love. I wish I could take my bird with me to the countryside. I vow, once you saw it, you would love it as I do!"

This I did not answer. I knew it was untrue, but I did not want to make her unhappy by saying so.

After breakfast I helped her bring her things down from our room, and then we hugged goodbye. She cried, but I did not, for I knew I would cry later, and she would not. My father carried her bundle, and walked with her to the inn where the coach would call. I stayed in the doorway, looking after them.

Susannah came and stood behind me. "Now it is just the two of us," she said. "And we will get on better."

But I did not answer.

The new lady's maid was called Joan. She was older and plainer and much finer than Hester, though she could not read, as Hester could. I thought I would hate her, but it was not so. The first night she found me reading by candlelight when she came to bed and said to me, "Read to me a bit before I sleep, won't you?" And I did, until I heard her snoring gently. After that we did so every night, unless she came late to bed from keeping company with Susannah while my father was out. By day she used a high, sweet voice, and petted my stepmother and fanned her and admired her. But at night, when her stays were undone at last, she sighed mightily and grinned at me before she fell into bed. Once she said, "This is nice. At my last place I slept on a truckle bed in the mistress's room." But in the main, we did not speak, except for my reading, which swiftly put her to sleep. She was larger than Hester, and when she slept her body gave off great heat, which was a comfort on cool nights.

Another good thing about Joan was that she sometimes kept Susannah from the shop. They went together to the Exchange to buy ribbons and pins, or to Drury Lane or Dorset Gardens to see the new plays performed, or to a card party given by a master goldsmith's wife. Usually my father would stay in the shop when she was gone, but once he left it to Robert and me to manage it between us. Trade was good that day, and I was proud to count the shillings into my father's hand at the end of it.

Yet, though I liked reading to Joan, and liked her taking Susannah from the shop once or twice in a week, nothing could make me like the ache I felt at missing Hester. For there was no one, now, to bandy words with me, or to make up foolish stories with me, or to pretend to scold me when I was too saucy, without meaning it one bit.

4

As the summer turned to autumn, we spent fewer mornings in the kitchen and more in the parlor, where Susannah taught me to do needlework. She did this, I was sure, because she knew how greatly I hated it. The kitchen had its warmth and its tasty pleasures, and even the stillroom had its curiosities, which made learning there of interest. But sitting near the fire with a needle, when I might have been helping in the shop or reading a book, was like poison to me. And while in the kitchen my clumsiness was feigned, with a needle I was truly clumsy. More than once I bled upon my work.

"Damme!" I exclaimed on one such occasion.

"Do not speak so," Susannah said, but she was not shocked.

"I do not see why I must learn turkey work. Of what use is it to me?"

"How can you ask? Only look at the fine carpet upon the table just there. I made that myself!"

I looked, not for the first time. It was truly a beautiful carpet, with a thick pile of green. The border that hung down around the table showed a forest of green trees and red deer browsing among them.

"Why can we not buy such things?" I asked, but I knew the answer. Carpets from Turkey or Persia were only for the rich.

We worked in silence for some time. Then I asked my stepmother what she was making.

"A christening cushion," she said, smiling down at her work. "See, this will be Moses in the bulrushes."

This answer roused my fury, for I knew she was thinking of the children she would bear my father. "I do not need to learn these arts," I said, and cast my work aside.

"Your husband will want you to know them."

"Husband! Who will marry me, now that you and the brats you will bear have taken away my inheritance?"

At last it was said. The knowledge that had parted us like a sword from the day she came into the house was spoken aloud. I could hardly believe what I had said: I expected her to rise, to scream, I expected thunder to peal, or the fire to die in the grate.

Instead, she spoke without looking at me. "That is why I am doing my best for you. For if you find no husband you will end up in service, and then your household arts will command you a better position."

For a moment I was without speech, and nearly without breath, as one who has had a sudden fall. Susannah looked up and saw my face, and her own filled with pity. She put down her needlework and put out her hand, as though to touch me, though she was not near enough.

I could feel the heat in my face, but my words were cool enough. "I see. I am being trained for service. Why did you not tell me from the start? It is always useful to learn a trade. However—I can find a better one, I vow."

And I left the room. She spoke to my back, but I knew not what she said. I went to my room and chased Joan from it. I threw myself upon the bed and cried, and bit my fist to stop myself, and then cried some more.

My father and stepmother supped together that night, while I ate with Joan in the small parlor. She was livelier at suppertime than at bedtime, and asked me many questions about the shop, and the famous men who came there. She told me about *The Rival Queens*, which was a play she had seen the King's Company perform at Drury Lane, and asked me if I had ever seen a play, but I had not. I gave her short answers, but she did not seem to mind. Then, as she began to tell me about beating Susannah at piquet, I cut into her talk with a question.

"How long have you been in service, Joan?"

"Twenty years this winter, it will be. I was fourteen when I took my first place."

"Why did you not marry?"

"I hadn't the fortune for it."

"And how is it—being in service?"

"Why, fine enough, if you've a good place. This one suits me, but it won't last long, I can tell."

"Why won't it?"

"When the babies come, your mother won't be wanting to be a woman of fashion anymore. It'll be nurses she wants, not lady's maids."

"I would not like to be in service," I said.

"Well, you've no need to be, I'm sure," Joan said in a comforting way, and helped herself to more tart.

I dreamed that night of Mr. Barker, the astrologer. We were on the Thames together in a little boat, and a storm was upon us. "That'll be two shillings," said the waterman who sat at the oars, but the boat began to spin and spin. "You must turn it *into the wind*!" Mr. Barker shouted, but the waterman did nothing. "I am speaking to you!" he shouted, and I saw that he meant me. "How can I turn it into the wind, when I am not at the oars?" I shouted back. Then I woke.

All that day I thought about how I might steer my boat into the wind, and when night fell, and my father and stepmother sat reading by the fire, I went to my father and stood before him.

"Sir, I would like to be apprenticed."

He took a moment to look up, as he always did, dragging his eyes from the page with an effort. Then he made me repeat what I had said, not having heard it. But Susannah had heard it. Her face was watchful as a rabbit's as she waited.

"Apprenticed?" he repeated, once he understood what I had said. "What can you mean, Margaret?"

"I would like you to sign articles, that I might be apprenticed. Another bookseller would be best, but anyone in a trade would do. A goldsmith. A cookshop. It doesn't matter. The money you get for my services will help with the wet nurses."

"I will not use a wet nurse," Susannah said quietly.

My father looked at her, then back at me. "Neither of you makes any sense. What nonsense is this, Meg? You need not serve an apprenticeship. You are to marry."

"No one will have me, now I have no fortune."

"You will have a suitable dowry."

"Shall I? Then why is your wife training me to be a servant in a fine home?"

"That is not what I said," Susannah said, but her face reddened as though with guilt.

"You will have a suitable dowry," my father said in a louder voice. "And if my wife has told you anything different, she is mistaken." He stood, holding his sheaf of pages carefully so as not to crease them. "And you *shall* have a wet nurse," he said more quietly to Susannah. Then he left the room.

"I will *not*," she said fiercely when he was gone. Then she looked up at me. "Why are you so cruel to me? Is it such a terrible thing to have a mother again?"

I could almost have pitied her, if she had not sent

Hester away. But she had. "I will not study with you any-more," I said.

"I thank God for it," she replied, and buried her face in her hands.

The next day I spent all day in the shop, and she did not. I was not happy, but I was satisfied.

AN ANTIDOTE AGAINST
MELANCHOLY

※ 1 ※

Robert liked my stepmother. I accused him of it one afternoon when the two of us had the shop together. My father and Susannah had gone to the Drydens' in Longacre to dine, and had not yet come back. Trade, which had been brisk for a little, had now died down. I tried to read, but the light was dim and gray, and besides, I was too out-of-sorts to stay interested in anything. I slapped my pages on the counter and went to stand in the open door of the shop. In the street, two of the Mr. Turners were talking together in a lively way. Robert said nothing. He was forever saying nothing, and it irritated me.

"I do not see why you fawn over my father's wife so," I said as I turned to him.

He did not look up from his ledger. He was recording the titles we had sold that day, and the shillings we had taken in. At last he said, "Because I am civil does not mean that I fawn. You ought to be civil yourself, you would get on better."

"You admire her."

He did not answer.

"Admit that you admire her," I demanded, advancing to his stool.

"There is no reason I should not admire her," he said, but did not stop his work.

It was as impossible to get conversation from him as it was to get honey from a pig, or ham from a bee. Conversation was not in his nature. But it was in mine, and there were some days I felt I would perish from keeping silent so much. I missed Hester even more than I had done when she first left, for then I spent my strength battling with Susannah. Now there was no ear for my wit, and none for my insults, either.

Just as I had this thought, my father and his wife came in from the street. They were talking to one another as they entered, and did not stop, as though they had not had chances enough to hear one another's words.

"I was shocked at Master Staley's jest," Susannah said as she cast back her hood. "He does not even try to hide that he is a Catholic."

"He will get himself into trouble one day," my father replied, shaking his head. He handed his walking stick to Robert, who left off writing to take it.

Susannah turned to me. "Good day, Meg. We have had a lively time of it at Mr. Dryden's. We must tell you all about it. Was there much trade?"

"Robert has the list," I said, and turned my back upon her.

There was a pause during which no one spoke. Then Susannah said, "You see?" and went through the door that led into the rest of the house.

My father was known as a pleasant man, who greeted all with a smile and avoided strong opinions as though they were strong drink. Some folk thrive on disaster, but my father throve on peace, plenty, and contentment. He liked a good dinner, and a good jest, and he wanted his wife and daughter to be pleasant together before the fire of an evening. But this he did not have.

The next day after dinner, my father said he had errands to do, and bade me roughly to come with him. Though I was eager enough to go with him, it angered me that he spoke so rough, when once he smiled so often. So I said only, "Yes, sir," without raising my eyes, and went for my cloak and hood.

It was early October, and the Michaelmas term was newly begun. The sun shone upon us as we left Little Britain, and the air was mild, with no chill. I turned to look at the wooden sign above our shop as we left it. On it was carved the shape of a five-pointed star. It had hung there long; I did not remember another. My father always said it was a lucky star. But I remembered talking with Hester about the comet, about whether the disasters it foretold were meant for us or for others. And I thought to myself that what is luck to one is not always luck to another.

We walked first through small streets, lanes where we had to kick the hens from our path, and then down larger ones, where our boot heels slipped into the wheel ruts of the coaches. I wondered where we were bound, but knew better than to ask. We passed a man selling turnips, and a woman selling lace. They both called out to us, and the woman called me pretty, which I am not, except that I have fine hair—long and brown, with red lights in it when the firelight glows—so Hester told me. But I could find no pleasure in sunshine nor in compliments.

We stretched our legs mightily that day. First my father bade me wait outside an apothecary's shop while he spoke to a man within. Then we went to the New Exchange, where we wandered through the arcade, looking at porcelain in one booth and hats in another. Before we left he bought me a ribbon and himself some gloves. Next we went to the printer, and he carried away the pages of a pamphlet against Catholics. At Lincoln's Inn Fields we paused a little, while we heard a woman sing a ballad about her man in the Fleet Prison, but she did not sing how he got there. At last we stopped by Will's. At the doorway I could see my father did not know whether to leave me outside or bring me within, but at last he made a motion to me. I followed him hastily through the door, lest he should change his mind, for I had heard often of Will's in Bow Street. It was said throughout the Town that all the cleverest wits sat before the fire there and traded jests. Mr. Dryden went there, and the Earl of Rochester, and the playwright Wycherley, and Aphra Behn. None of them was there the afternoon that I entered with my father, but I did not care.

Inside there was a great din. The tables were crowded with men drinking and smoking, arguing so vehemently that their wig curls danced, or shouting with loud laughter. Their voices vied with one another; they thumped their tankards on the tables or pounded their spoons upon their plates to make a point. The fire made the room too hot and the air too smoky, and the smells of pipe tobacco and coffee filled my nostrils. I pulled at my cloak to let the air in while my father bent over a man at the nearest table and shouted a question at him.

My father was looking for a man named Brown, who was to write for him a book on geometry for seamen. He did not find him, but not finding him took twenty minutes while he exchanged pleasantries with a man named Greene, who had written a bad play that no one would publish, and twenty more while he spoke with a physician named White, who would not write his recipes into a book for my father, no matter what he was promised. I thought twice of things I might say, but held my tongue between my teeth instead, lest my father should send me back to the street. But for near an hour I was happy again, awake, alive, loving London and books and talk. At last, however, my father turned and left, and I, like seaweed, trailed in his wake, remembering my cares and letting them show on my face.

"There, that's the book trade for you," he said when we were outside once more.

"Not for me," I said in a mutter. I intended that he should not hear me, but I half hoped that he would.

He did, and did not like what he heard.

"If this life becomes you so ill, you needn't live it," he said.

I stared at him, wondering if he meant I should take my own life.

"I am sick to death of this unhappiness at my hearth," he went on. "If you are so miserable, go to where you'll be less so. Hester and her family would be glad enough of your help in the country. Perhaps it would be the best place for you."

He had begun to walk again, quickly, heading back toward the sign of the Star. I could not keep up with him, but scrambled after him. I heard his words but could scarcely credit them; they were like an axe that shatters the frozen river in winter, and sends glimmering shards flying everywhere, and reveals the dark, cold, angry water beneath.

"You are sending me away?" I asked at last, running to catch him up.

He stopped and looked down at me, and then looked over my head again, at the timbered shop behind. "If you cannot get along with your mother, aye, then you must go away. If you will make your peace with her, and wear a smile again and keep a friendly tongue in your head instead of a sour one, then you may stay. You are a help to me, Margaret, when you choose to be."

Angry words swelled in me but I dared not speak them.

I do not know what showed in my face: it may have been anger, or it may have been fear, or it may simply have been the horrible hurt it gave me that my father wanted to send me away.

"You need not decide now, Meg. Think of it for a few days, nay, a week, even two, and tell me your choice then. It is not an easy choice. I offer it for your sake, that you need not be unhappy."

I did not believe him. I did not answer him. I walked by his side through London, toward the sign of the Star, where all my fortunes had come undone.

❧ 2 ❧

At first there was only the shock of being told by my own father that I would be sent away if I did not mend my ways. It was not a thing I ever thought to hear from him. So many feelings warred within me, I knew not which was true. But I suppose they were all true.

I felt a terrible anger at my stepmother's power, and at my father's injustice.

I felt a deep grief that my father, the man who once gave me his pipe to hold while I sat upon his knee, could now live so easily without me.

I felt an anxiety that was almost like terror at the thought of seeing London no more, of hearing no longer the clamor of the streets and the chatter of the shop.

And I felt a yearning for Hester, who was perhaps the

only person in the world who loved me. I imagined walking home with her from the village church, laughing about the curate's bald head. And I thought: perhaps that is the fate I will choose. Then my eye would light upon a book of essays or a printed sermon and I would think: no, I can't. I can't.

Because I knew not how to choose, I became cautious in my speech and manner, that I might keep all doors open. I began to school myself in cheerful habits, in smiling when I felt like scowling, in asking civil questions when I cared nothing for the answers.

The first time I asked my stepmother how she slept I thought she would drop the mug she drank from. Indeed, it did bobble in her hands, and drops of ale fell upon her skirt. She wiped at them with a hand while she stared at me. "I slept well, thank you," she said at last. "And you?"

"Oh, I always sleep well now that Joan warms the bed," I said with a laugh. My stepmother laughed, too, and just then my father passed by and heard our laughter. This satisfied me and yet angered me, for I did not like to be bending to his will. The smile went from my mouth and as soon as my father was gone I got up and left the room in haste.

I did not change my ways all at once. For hours upon end I was as sullen as ever. But each day I tried to be nice to my stepmother at least one time. And each time I was nice to her, she smiled with such surprise and delight that for a moment it shamed me to be only pretending niceness. Then I would remind myself that it was she who had sent Hester from me.

One Sunday in late October I went with my father and mother to dine at the home of Philip Gosse, who was a wine merchant in the City, and his family. This visit had been talked of for some time, for Susannah had been long acquainted with the family, and thought I should know them. This was on account of their daughter Anne, who was fifteen. By Susannah's account, Anne was all that a daughter should be: skilled at women's arts, and helpful in the care of her younger brothers and sisters. I had seen her at the wedding but did not like her; I thought she would be silly and dull. Before my father threatened to send me away, however, I looked forward to meeting her, simply that I might make sly remarks which would confuse or shock her. But now I dared nothing, so I dreaded meeting Anne Gosse. I vowed I would sit silent and smiling all the visit, so that afterward the Gosse family would wonder to each other if my mind was not quite sound.

But it was not like that.

When we came into the room where Anne sat with her mother she was surrounded by her brothers and sisters. It was a large room, with a bright wood fire and a map of England mounted upon the wall. A little boy buried his head beneath Anne's apron and giggled whilst she tickled him, and a little girl tugged at her sleeve for attention, and an even smaller child tried to pull himself up on her skirt, but did not succeed, and plopped down on his bottom once more.

"Hush, hush, our guests have come," Anne said when she saw us, and patted and smoothed the children, and then herself, as she smiled at us. She had had the smallpox, and her face was sorely pitted, but she had a lovely smile with good teeth, and a knot of fine, glossy dark hair upon her neck.

"Anne, this is my daughter, Margaret, who has long wanted to meet you," Susannah said when I had been introduced to Mrs. Gosse. "She is hoping you will show her some of your embroidery."

"Oh, may I?" said Anne. "I am very vain about it, I confess. I have just done the most lovely thing, all peacocks and grass. It was an enormous labor."

I stared at her, for I had never heard a girl boast so.

"I'll get it, I'll get it," cried the little girl, and ran off. Susannah left, too, with Anne's mother, and Anne and I sat down together on stools near the fire.

"I did that seat cover," Anne said, just as I lowered my bottom onto a huntsman and two deer.

"You're very skilled," I said politely.

"It took me forever to learn, you cannot imagine. My mother laughed at me, and said I would never be a needlewoman and had better darn and spin. But I was determined. Determination wins all prizes, does it not?"

I gave my head a quick shake in spite of myself, and tears came to my eyes. For it was not my experience that determination won all prizes.

I do not know if she saw my tears. But she said, "No, I suppose not. I wish it did, however."

I felt an odd sensation on my knee, and looked to see a tiny hand there. The baby had pulled himself to stand using my stool, and now grasped my skirts.

"Tom, Tom, this is our guest!" Anne said, reaching toward him.

"No, please—let him stay," I said. I reached out and petted his soft cheek with a finger. His face was plump under its white bonnet, and his eyes were brown and bright. "How old is he?" I asked.

"Nine months. He is the latest—and last, we all hope! For my mother has done her part—there are ten of us. I am the eldest. And though she is strong, and has lost but two, there is much to fear when a woman comes to childbed."

"But where does he suckle? Why is he not in the country with a wet nurse?"

"My mother does not stand for it, not anymore. She says they are more likely to die if they are sent away."

Just then the little girl came in with a runner draped over her arms. It was indeed beautiful. The stitches seemed to shine in the afternoon sunlight that came through the drawing room window.

"Thank you, Jenny," Anne said, and then to me: "I know you do not really want to see my work. Why should you? But I am so proud, I must show you."

So we bent over her work together, while Tom clutched at my knees and Jenny stuck her head in my way.

"You see this stitch, here in the eye of the peacock's tail? It was very difficult, I cannot tell you how difficult. I had to begin anew a dozen times. My father vowed he would buy me no more thread, but of course he did not mean it. Thomas, no!" For the baby was crumpling her work in his little hand.

I pried his tiny fingers from the cloth and lifted him into my arms. He was round and light, like good bread. His little white dress floated around him as I lifted him.

"How lucky you are to have a brother," I said.

"He is so precious! But they are all precious. It's a hardship on my father that we are so many, but I mean to have as many myself when I marry, if I am strong enough. And you, do you want many children?"

"I will take what I am given, I suppose," I said. "What is the good of wanting things when we have no choices? I would rather spend my time selling books than raising babies, but I suppose my fate will be like that of every woman."

Anne looked at me a moment, considering. "No one can force you to marry," she said at last. "It is not lawful."

"There is so much more than law that binds us," I answered her.

"You read much, I can tell. Tell me about your father's shop, and what you do there?"

Then I spoke of the trade, and of listening to Mr. Dryden and Mr. Wycherley speak on poetical subjects, and of lingering at Will's. I spoke slowly at first, but she listened with great attention to all I said, and asked many questions. It had been long since anyone cared to hear me talk, and as I spoke I felt like a stream that has shrunk to a trickle during the dry months, and now swells with the first rainfall. Anne Gosse seemed to know little of her father's business or any other; she was concerned only with women's things. But I did not care. It was a fine, fine thing to have conversation once more!

The little boy, who had gone from the room, presently came back with an older sister.

"Play with me!" he begged Anne.

"No, let us do some acrostics," the sister, who was perhaps nine, suggested.

Anne shook her head. "Take Charlie away, please, Gertrude," she said. She kissed Charlie's cheek. "We'll play Hunt-the-Slipper after dinner, won't we? Right now Margaret and I must talk."

"You may call me Meg," I said to her.

She smiled at me, a wide, bright smile. "Sometimes they call me Annie," she said. "I don't mind it."

We talked and we talked. She was a glad, cheerful girl, who laughed at all my jokes. Jesting with her made me think of Hester, and I missed her with a sharp ache, and reminded myself: I can go to her if I like.

The Gosse house was larger and grander than ours. In the dining room hung a portrait of the King in a rich gilt frame, the finest I had ever seen. Around the great table there were walnut chairs with velvet backs, so many that not one grown person sat on a bench or a stool while we ate. Dinner was very fine, with four courses, and baked bananas for dessert. I ate until my stomach ached inside its lacings. Gertrude was the youngest child at table; the younger children were fed elsewhere. But Anne's brothers were there: stout, loud, red-faced boys of fourteen and thirteen who talked mainly to each other, teasing one another with riddles or setting puzzles in arithmetic.

After dinner, when the last comfits were eaten, we all stood in a ring in the largest parlor and played Hunt-the-Slipper. Anne and I were next to one another, and passed the slipper slyly along behind our backs while Susannah sought for it, but at last she found it when it came to little Jenny, who forgot what she was to do. Then it was Jenny's turn, but Anne came into the center of the ring with her and they hunted together for the slipper. There was much laughter, and I saw why Anne so enjoyed being part of a large family. At last, however, the children tired, and began to quarrel, and so were sent away. Then Anne and I were at liberty to talk once more.

"It has been such fun to have you here," she said to me. "I seldom see other girls, for Mother says there are quite enough of us without inviting yet more children into the house." I opened my mouth to say something pretty in reply, but she went on, "Sometimes I am afraid I will be married young, simply because there are too many of us at home."

"I'm sure you need not think of it yet," I said to comfort her.

"I know, I know! I am too young to think of it, my mother is always saying so. And yet, *they* think of it. I hear them when they think I am abed or busy with my needle, speaking of this merchant or that. There are so many of us, you know, and so many girls. I haven't the dowry I'd like, and as you see I am not beautiful."

She did not look at me as she spoke, and though her voice was matter-of-fact, I could tell that her scarred face troubled her. I wondered how old she had been when it happened.

"So," she continued in a bright, false voice. "They will pick someone old, who will take my youth as a marriage portion."

"I'm sorry," I said.

Her smile faded. Then she said, very seriously, "Perhaps I will be lucky, like Susannah, who married your father."

At that moment my father came into the room with his bride on his arm. His cheeks were red from port, and his smile was broad as he turned to Susannah. I looked at her, and saw that her smile was not so broad. I wondered for the first time if she had wanted him, or if she merely did her duty.

❧ 3 ❧

One day at breakfast time Susannah said to my father, "You can spare me from the shop, can you not? I had thought to take Margaret to the New Spring Garden at Vauxhall today."

"Cannot—" I said quickly, and then stopped myself. I meant to say, "Cannot Joan go with you instead?" For I did not want to wander among bushes when I might be in the shop with my father. But I dared not speak my thoughts. I looked down at my breakfast platter, which that morning bore buttered bread and oysters. "Might Anne Gosse come with us?" I asked with little hope.

"No doubt Anne is needed to help her mother," my father replied. "Theirs is a busy household."

"It will not hurt to ask," Susannah said. "We will send Godfrey with a message. It will give Mrs. Gosse kind feelings toward us, even if she cannot spare Anne." She began to speak of the beauties of Vauxhall, but she could not interest me. I did not want to go there, unless indeed Anne could come with us, but that seemed scarcely likely.

However, the stars must have been well aligned for me that day, for Anne's mother let her go with us after all, and suddenly, instead of feeling cross, I felt alive with my good luck. Anne was as excited as I. There were four of us in the boat that took us down the Thames, for Joan came as well, of course. I have always loved the river, and had not been upon it for more than a year, so I settled myself happily next to Anne and watched the man at the oars with rapt attention. His muscles flexed and strained as he rowed. The wind mussed our hair and reddened our cheeks, and drops of cold river water flew through the air and landed upon our skirts, and the watermen, who were famous for their jesting, teased us and asked us if we had gallants we were meeting secretly at Vauxhall. It was glorious.

And the gardens! The gardens were lovely. The weather

was fine. I believe it was the last fine day that year, and the air was soft and warm on the cheek, as though it remembered summer. The breeze sang in the trees, and golden leaves dropped from the arbors even as we passed under them. There were still a few flowers in surprising patches of crimson or purple. Anne and I walked arm-in-arm, trailing behind Susannah and Joan. First we exclaimed about the beauty of the place—it was her first time there as well as mine—but before long we fell into confidences, as I had hoped we would. I told her everything—that my stepmother and I did not get on well, and that my father had given me this cruel choice.

"I did not know she was so hard a woman," Anne said in a low voice, so that Susannah and Joan might not hear. "She has always been kind to me. Does she beat you?"

"My father would not let her!" I answered.

"In what way does she show her cruelty, then?"

"She is not cruel. But she will not let me be who I am. She tries to make me into someone else, into someone who embroiders cushions and bakes tarts."

"Into a woman, you mean," Anne said, laughing gently. "But you *will* be a woman someday, Meg. Is that so bad a thing?"

"My mother was a woman. Aphra Behn is a woman. That sort of woman I do not mind becoming. But I do not want to become Susannah Beckwith."

"You will not, I can assure you," Anne said with a smile. "You need not fly to the country to avoid such a fate."

I saw that I had lost her sympathy, and struggled to regain it. "She sent Hester away from me. I cannot forgive her."

Her smile faded. "There is no injury like the loss of one you love."

"I miss her terribly."

Anne squeezed my arm. "Perhaps, then, you should go to Surrey after all."

Just then the lane we followed met another. Susannah and Joan waited where the paths crossed, and Susannah pointed to a tree that was hung with lamps. "At night the lamps are lit," she said. "There are hundreds. It is very bright on the main paths, bright as day!"

I heard a lark sing. Its song was very sweet and rich. I imagined myself with Hester in the countryside, eating red apples from the tree and listening to birdsong, and I felt tears standing in my eyes. Could the country be so bad a fate?

We began to walk again, and once more we fell behind. Anne and I walked in silence for a time. We could hear Susannah and Joan chattering together, and every now and then caught a few words. "So hard to please," Susannah said once, and Joan said, "Time will tell."

"Of course," Anne said after a while, "I suppose in the country you will cook and sew every bit as much as in London, though you are more apt to darn stockings than to embroider cushions. But you will be with Hester."

I did not reply. I saw myself in a Surrey cottage, huddled near a coal fire too poor to keep off the winter draft.

I saw myself peering at the stocking pulled over my hand, holding my needle uncertainly aloft. *It will not be like that*, I thought, and tried to picture myself eating apples with Hester once again, but somehow I could not keep the autumn chill away from us as we ate.

The lane turned once more, and suddenly I heard a sound that was not a bird. 'Twas a fiddle, for a man stood where two pathways crossed and played his instrument as we passed by. And I do not mean to say that man can make a better sound than the birds who were blessed by God with such happy throats, yet I never heard such sweet notes as these that climbed and fell and *opened* somehow under the sky. I was so struck, I stood for a moment, staring at him, and Anne looked back at me in surprise.

"Come, Meg," she said, but Susannah said, "No, it's what we've come for."

And I thought: Why go to the country, when one can live in London and go to Vauxhall?

At last we walked on, but there was ever music following us, sometimes birdsong and sometimes a fiddle or a harp, and then we came to a pavilion where there was much dancing. We sat nearby and ate our beef pasties, and Joan and Susannah had wine. When we were done, we danced, Susannah with Joan and I with Anne. And then Susannah said that we would trade partners, and held out her hand to me. I remembered the wedding, and how I would not dance there because I did not like my stepmother. But now the music was so lively and my spirits were so light that I could not help myself. We joined the crowd and swept round the pavilion with our skirts whirling until we panted and could dance no more.

On the way home we were all of us tired and quiet. The weather had begun to grow cold, and we pulled our cloaks around ourselves in the boat. We walked with Anne to her house, and as she kissed me goodbye she whispered, "Send me word of your decision."

After we left Anne at her house and were headed toward Little Britain, Susannah said to me, "It is not so bad to have a mother again, is it?"

All the pleasure of the day fled. I did not know how to answer her. I wanted to say, "You are not my mother." Or even: "Do not make me like you." But I found I could not speak, and instead only smiled a faint, false smile.

⊰ 4 ⊱

It was on the Tuesday next that Mr. Winter came into the shop for the first time in several weeks. Now that there were no lessons in the kitchen, I spent most mornings with Robert at a bookstall in St. Paul's Churchyard, and my afternoons with my father in the shop. Once more it was I who took Paul Winter's coin when he came to read, for he rarely came before three or four of the clock.

"Good afternoon, Meg," he said to me that day as he entered. "What are you reading today?"

"Nothing, sir. I only amuse myself," I said, and lowered my book so he could not see it, for I was reading only jests and ballads, and I knew he would have no great opinion of them.

"Amusement is not a vice. Show me what you read, Meg."

I held it out to him, and he turned over the clean page and read the title aloud. "*An Antidote Against Melancholy, Made Up in Pills. Compounded of Witty Ballads, Jovial Songs, and Merry Catches.* Well." He handed back the pages. "I hope you are not truly melancholy, that you need such an antidote."

"Certainly not, sir," I said, but he looked at me keenly and I knew he thought I lied.

"Do the songs cheer you?"

"They do, sir."

"Show me your favorite."

I had no special favorite, so I read him out a riddle.

" 'He went to the wood and he caught it,/He sat him down and he sought it,/Because he could not find it,/Home with him he brought it.' Well, Mr. Winter, what do you suppose the man caught?"

"Hmmm." Mr. Winter thought. "Because he couldn't find it he had to bring it home . . . a tick, perhaps?"

"A thorn."

"Ah, a thorn. That has happened to me. Riddles are good fun. Is there another you like?"

"Not a riddle, no . . . but I like the song between Nanny

and Jenny, where they sing of their sweethearts, and why they will not marry. The Baker stinks of sweat, you see, from working at the ovens, and the Butcher is too bloody, and the Tailor too poor . . . the early verses are very witty, though later they begin to be too much like each other. I think they ought to have made a verse about a sexton, that would have given good fun."

"Perhaps you should write one yourself."

"I?" I tried to laugh, but I could feel myself turning pink, as though caught at something, for in truth I had tried my hand at just such a verse, but my attempt was a failure. I spoke quickly, to change the subject. "At last Jenny sings that she will never marry . . . but I suppose she will be very poor if she does not, and will live always in her brother's house, sweeping up after his wife and taking care of his children."

In my hurry to change the subject I spoke of what I did not mean to say. I looked away from him, hoping that he did not understand what lay beneath my words. But he did understand, and drummed his fingers against the counter as he thought of it.

"Nanny and Jenny had better marry booksellers," he said at last.

"Perhaps they had not dowry enough."

"You must not worry so, Meg. Everything will come right."

"How can you make such a promise, when there are so many for whom things go so wrong?"

"I trust your father, that is why. He will not fail in his duty to you. Do you not trust him?"

"I trust him, yes, but . . . I am no longer the only one he loves. I am not the only one to whom he owes a duty. I wish . . ."

"What do you wish, Margaret?"

"I wish my fate lay in my own hands."

"That is true for none of us."

"But for a man it is more true than for a woman."

"Yes, that is so—for some men. Not for Robert, who must serve your father until his contract has been fulfilled. Not for Julius, the African who waits upon Sir William; he may be sold to another at any moment."

"My father . . ."

"Is at the mercy of circumstances, as are we all. It is true there are some choices he can make. But . . . there are strong women who take their fates in their own hands, you know. There are women who preach, women who teach, women who act upon the stage, women who write, women who sell books, women who brew ale. They are free, though I do not know that they are happy . . . I think few are who travel life's road alone."

"*You* travel life's road alone."

He smiled and shook his head. "Nay, Meg, I do not," he said. "I have many friends who travel it with me."

I thought often after that conversation of what he had said of these women, women who preached and taught. Of course I could not do those things. I had no education.

I could sell books, certainly . . . but only if I first married a bookseller, and inherited his rights upon his death. I did not think I could brew ale even if I married a brewer and learned all he knew; the smell alone would be too strong for me.

I did wonder, a little, about women who wrote. But I thought to myself that to make oneself independent that way would be nearly impossible. I knew of no woman who had done it, saving only Aphra Behn.

❧ 5 ❧

One evening as I sat in the small parlor, helping Joan with the mending, my father came to me and said, "Well, Meg, have you made your choice?"

I knew well what he meant, but pretended for a moment that I did not. "My choice, sir?" I asked him.

Joan murmured something about thread and left the room.

"If you are to go to Surrey you must travel now, before the winter is upon us."

"Do you want me to go, Father?" I asked and I knew he heard the pain in my voice.

He looked surprised. "No, of course not, Meg. I would rather you stay with us. Susannah prefers it, too. But I have told her it is to be your choice. I would not have you unhappy."

I thought of my words to Mr. Winter, that I wanted to have my own fate in my own hands, and thought: I do. At least in this. It was true for very few, especially among children. Yet I was one of these.

"Thank you," I said to my father, and tears spilled suddenly down my cheeks.

"You choose to go, then?" he asked, and the heaviness in his voice filled me with joy.

"No, sir. If it pleases you, I will stay with you in London."

He stooped and kissed me on the brow. "It pleases me, Daughter," he said, and left the room.

I sat with a torn apron in my lap and could not keep the tears from coming. Joan came back in and said, "What, are you melancholy again? And I thought you were feeling better these past weeks."

Everyone thought so. I had grown quite used to pretending I was happy when I was not. I smiled at Susannah when I passed her in the hall, and murmured my dismay when she bumped her elbow on the wooden cabinet in the parlor. I told riddles to Joan, and even to my father. I sang a little while I packed the books Robert and I would sell at St. Paul's Churchyard, songs that were out of season, about Maying or midsummer. My father heard me and hushed me, but with a wink, the way he used to do when he was proud of my wit but did not want to show it.

What puzzled me was, the more I pretended to be happy the happier I indeed felt. Nothing had changed. My father had still chosen his bride over me, Hester was still gone, my inheritance was still gone, my fortunes remained uncertain.

And yet it was not so very hard to sing, and once or twice I did so without plan.

SIR PATIENT FANCY

❧ 1 ❧

The day after I told my father of my decision I sent our boy Godfrey to the Gosse house with a two-word message to Anne: *I stay*. And the truth of those two words gave me more satisfaction than I had imagined that I could feel at the prospect of staying on in my stepmother's household.

Susannah was pleased, too, that I had chosen to stay in London, which did not surprise me. She knew I would be a great help to her when her babies began arriving, at least, if they lived. And she may have thought that it meant that I had chosen at last to love her. That I could not do. But there were moments I almost loved her without choosing it.

One of those was the day she told my father she meant to invite the Gosse family for Christmas.

Before my mother died, Christmastide was always marvelous at our house, with the most delicious treats, the brightest lights, the most fragrant green boughs brought from the countryside to decorate the hearth, the sweetest carols sung. I remember well the last Christmas she lived, how my mother labored late into the night baking mince pies, and how I woke her early the next morning because I could not sleep for excitement. She cuffed me for waking her, and began to scold, then suddenly she hugged me instead, and bade me be merry all the day. And I was, for she was carrying then, and I hoped for a little brother or sister when the spring came.

But instead the spring brought only death, and since that time my father would not celebrate Christmas at home. We never dressed the house, nor made mince pies, nor asked company in. Instead we went always to someone else's house, and that someone was often a man, and childless. Last Christmas we had gone to the house of Titus Woods, my father's uncle. He spent the day telling me how lucky I was to have been born in the reign of Charles II, and how he himself had grown up under Puritan rule, and was not allowed to have Christmas. Then he told me of all his neighbors, and which ones were Puritans in their hearts, though he had seen them that morning at St. Mary-le-Bow. At last, however, he fell to talking of bowls with my father, and I was allowed to help the servants clear the table. I almost wished we had stayed at home.

So when Susannah said at supper one evening that she would ask the Gosse family for Christmas Day, I looked up from my plate to see what my father might say.

" 'Tis an enormous bother to have guests for Christmas," he answered her, hardly pausing between his bites of roast mutton.

"Why, you need not worry about the bother, you have a wife now."

"Meg and I have got out of the habit of it. I believe my uncle may ask us to dine."

"Don't be foolish," Susannah said briskly. " 'Twould be more fitting if he were to dine with us."

He put his fork down and looked at her for a moment without speaking, and I knew he could think of no more excuses. "No," he said at last. "No, it pleases me not."

I felt a quick sting of tears, which surprised me, for I had not known how much I wanted to have a merry Christmas once more.

But Susannah was not finished. "Miles," she said, putting a hand upon his shoulder. "Are we not a family? Is that not why you married, to leave those lonely Christmases behind you?"

"Do not speak so," he said roughly, and he strode from the room, leaving his supper unfinished upon the table.

"You have offended him," I burst out in dismay.

"We shall see," Susannah said calmly as she helped herself to a radish from my father's plate.

And the next afternoon she told me that the Gosse family would indeed be our guests on Christmas Day.

Christmas was almost upon us. My father grumbled much because every tradesman had his box set out and expected a little something for the season, so he spent an extra penny when he had his shoes repaired and tuppence when he brought a goose home from the cookshop. "I will have nothing left for presents," he said, but we did not believe him.

I had little money to spend this year, for Susannah now had charge of the household accounts. But I had saved the change a few times when Cook sent me out for a flounder or some turnips, so I bought oranges and tobacco for my father, and for my stepmother I made violet cakes, just as she had taught me.

On Christmas Eve, Susannah and I spent long hours in the kitchen making mince pies with Cook, Jane, and Joan. I was so tired Christmas morning that I could barely rouse myself, but did, and we all went off to St. Botolph's to hear Reverend Little make even the Incarnation dull. However, we were surprised, for Dr. Rolph preached instead, and I caught from him the excitement of Christmas, and wondered if Dr. Rolph had written his sermons up for any of the booksellers.

Then home, where we made ready for the Gosse family. Though our house was not so grand as theirs, it was indeed beautiful that day, for it was filled with fragrant green boughs and red berries, and the smells of good things roasting. Dozens of bright candle flames were reflected in the looking glasses, and all seemed magic.

The Gosse family arrived in two hackney coaches, for they would not all fit in one. They tumbled through the door laughing and teasing one another, filled with such good humor that the house seemed to grow warmer at once. Anne was friendly and outspoken, as always. She was so very immodest in her speech that Dr. Allestree, who wrote *The Ladies' Calling*, would surely have called her brazen. "I have heard the most scandalous story!" she declared as we sat down upon stools in the parlor. "About Mistress Barry and Betty Boutel, the actresses. Have you seen them? One has stabbed the other with a sword, onstage, whilst all watched! I do not remember which was stabbed, but they say she is not badly hurt. I wish I had been there!"

Whereupon I confessed that I had never seen a play.

"Have you not? It is great fun! Surely your father will allow it, he is such a literary man. I know Reverend Little says it is a vice, but he means it is a vice to go every day, or twice a day, and spend all one's time there, seeing the same plays over and over and talking through them with your friends. So many people do that! It is indeed a monstrous waste of time and money. But really, there are some very good morals put upon the boards, and"—she colored as she spoke, and her eyes grew bright—"there are some very funny things which are less moral, I confess."

"Those are the best, I vow," her brother Henry said.

I was startled to find him behind me, and drew my skirts to me as though he were a pickpocket. He grinned to see me alarmed.

"Meg has never been to the playhouse," Anne said.

"What, never? It's great fun. Why, I've seen Dryden and Wycherley and Shakespeare and Etheredge and ever so many others."

"I have read them," I said, to excuse myself.

"What, read them all!"

"A great many."

"If that's how you choose to spend your time," he scoffed, and went to find his brother.

I did not care what he said, but all the same I felt stupid for never having seen a play, and vowed I would make my stepmother take me to one as soon as Christmastide was over.

Susannah had worried herself much over dinner, but everyone enjoyed it greatly. As well as the mince pies, we had turkey stuffed with cloves, much plum porridge, pickled lime-buds, and oysters stewed in white wine. Afterward Anne and I took care of the children while our parents made merry at cards. And when that was done we all walked awhile upon the leads, that is, over the flat parts of the rooftops. Joan stayed at home to help the nurse with the children who were too little to go with us. But Anne, and her brothers, and I, too, went with our elders, and looked down at the sign of the Star swinging in the wind.

Anne and I walked with our cloaks wrapped tight around us, for the air was chill and sharp. We trailed behind the grown women, pausing now and then to look down into the street and exclaim upon a coach going by, or an idle apprentice who leaned against a shop wall.

"How do you fare, Meg? I suppose Mrs. Moore has forced you to labor over the mince pies when you wished you had been reading?" Anne asked.

I knew that she was laughing at me but it did not

prickle, for her smile was warm and merry. "I do not mind helping with mince pies at Christmas time!" I replied. "Somebody must make them."

"And they were perfectly done, so you may be proud."

"My stepmother may be proud. I but did her bidding. I know you are more skilled than I at such matters. How do you fare yourself? It is a busy season, I know."

"Very busy, and my father's business is good. Everyone in London wants extra wine at Christmastide. He does his business chiefly away from home, so we have seen little of him of late. But I have had much fun with the children."

I looked sideways at her. Her eyes were bright and her dark brown ringlets danced in the wind as we walked. "Then you are happy?" I asked.

She hesitated. "I am happy on those days when my fear of the future does not steal away my joy. I will be sixteen soon. And you?"

"I will be thirteen on the Feast of St. Valentine."

"But, are you happy?"

"I am like you, happy when I do not fear the future." I did not add that those days were very few.

"Most days I am happy indeed," Anne continued. "But then, I am so lucky."

I turned so quickly to look at her that I stumbled over the shingles, and she gripped my arm tightly and bade me be more careful. "Lucky?" I repeated. For I did not see how she could say so. With her small dowry and her pitted face she was placed even more unfortunately than I was.

"Yes, of course. I am so fortunate that both my parents

live, and that I have so many brothers and sisters, and that the wine business thrives and we have all we need."

"Yes, you have had good fortune there," I said, thinking of my own mother's death.

"I am so sorry, Meg," she said, and I could see she knew my thoughts. "But now you have a mother again, and perhaps soon a brother or sister, and you will be lucky, too!" And she squeezed my arm.

I could not answer her, but she did not notice. I liked Anne Gosse, but I marveled that she understood so little of my situation, or of her own. I suppose that is the good of expecting so little of life; it is easy to be contented when little comes.

But I do not expect little of life.

After supper the fiddlers came, and played late into the night while we all danced. The neighbors came, too, and several of our authors, and I did not think about whether or not I was lucky, but danced and laughed and felt bright and glad as though all my cares had gone.

2

It was a merry time. Children came round singing carols every night, bearing a wassail bowl with them. Dr. Rolph was at St. Botolph's all week, and we heard a fine sermon from him on St. John's Day, and another on New Year's Day, when bells rang all through London Town with a joyous sound. On Twelfth Night we had a pot of chocolate at breakfast, and in the evening went to the home of Colonel Woods. There we had fiddling and dancing and cakes and ale, and a King and Queen were chosen. Everyone was foolish and full of laughter. I stayed awake very late, much later than Hester would have let me do, and had great fun.

But the next morning all the merriment was over. We began to have gray, drizzling days, and long, long nights. I thought of what Anne had said about seeing a play, and wanted to ask Susannah if I might go with her some time, but I hardly dared to speak of it, for she seemed always cross these days. If I tried to read by firelight she scolded me and said I would ruin my eyes, and if I tried to read by candlelight she said I wasted the wick. I wondered what ailed her, and my father wondered, too.

We were in the shop, all three of us, when he asked her outright. There were no customers near, but Robert was there, and she had just scolded him for putting some old almanacs into a box, which my father himself had told Robert to do. "Nothing pleases you of late," he said to her. "What ails you?"

"Nothing, I am only bored. Every day is the same."

This was so untrue that I looked at her with open mouth, and then at my father. But he did not seem surprised.

"Why do you not have some friends to play cards with you?" he suggested.

"Or go to the playhouse," I said suddenly.

They both turned to stare at me.

"And take me with you," I said. "I have never been."

"It is bad enough to have my wife waste her time so, without my daughter wasting hers as well," my father said, but I saw that he did not mean it. He only wanted to rouse Susannah, for he liked her argument more than her boredom.

"Let us hope John Dryden does not hear you say so," Susannah answered sharply, and he laughed.

"Will you take her to see something of Dryden's, then?" he asked.

In my eagerness I burst out without thinking. "Please, Mother . . . may I see what Aphra Behn does next?" I asked.

Again they stared at me.

"What do you know of Mrs. Behn?" Susannah asked with disapproval.

My father made a scoffing noise. "In this family, how could she not know of Mrs. Behn? She knows of everything, Meg does. She is practically one of the Town wits."

He was bragging about me. It had been a long while since I had heard him brag about me, and it made me so happy that I kept quiet, and it was well I did.

"That woman has no modesty," Susannah said. "She writes every bit as bawdy as a man."

"Well, you need not ask her to a card party," my father said. "It will do Meg no more harm to see a bawdy play writ by a woman than one writ by a man, I suppose."

"You cannot mean that you want me to take her to a bawdy play."

"She reads them, does she not? Tell the truth, Margaret, have you read bawdy plays? Have you read Wycherley's plays?"

"Yes, Father."

"Well, you must stop such reading right now. I will find you something more wholesome," my stepmother said.

"You cannot stop a clever child from reading. My father could not stop me, and he used a rod. Let her read what she likes, and see what she likes, too," he said.

"But, Miles—"

"She is my child," he said, almost angrily, and she closed her mouth with a snap, as though she were a turtle.

You would not think that arguing with my father would make her mood happy but somehow it seemed to do so. For the next few days Susannah was more like herself, brisk and well occupied and contented. Then my father came into the shop and said to me, "Mrs. Behn has written a new play. It will open next week at Dorset Gardens."

For a moment I could not answer, only look at him with hope. At last I ventured, "Does my mother care to see it?"

He smiled slyly. "I have made her care."

From that day I grew so excited I could barely read. Susannah was not happy about going to see one of Mrs. Behn's plays, but when she saw my excitement she softened a little.

"What must I wear?" I asked Susannah, and then she softened more, for I seldom asked for her advice, or cared what I wore.

"You shall wear what you did for our wedding," she

replied. "Your very best." Then she spoke of the fine ladies I would see there, and the bright dresses they would wear, and the patches of moons and suns and stars they would have on their faces. Of course I had seen fine ladies before, but in truth, I had never looked at them overmuch. Now, for the first time, I felt an interest.

"And will you wear patches?" I asked Susannah, for I had never seen her do so.

She laughed. "Nay, I am a simple woman," she said.

3

We saw *Sir Patient Fancy* on January 17. It was a dark day and the air was damp all morning, and by the time we sat down to our pigeon pie it was beginning to rain.

My father took a long look out the window, then sat down at last. "You had better go another day," he said. "Your finery will be ruined."

"But if the play closes?" I cried out.

"Then see another play. London is full of plays, my girl."

"Father, please!"

"Don't vex me, child. What think you, Susannah?"

"That Godfrey and Jane have gone already to the playhouse to hold our seats," she said, and broke into her pie with a spoon.

After dinner Joan helped us to dress. She had put my hair in curl papers, and it took forever to arrange my ringlets. Then she tried the sleeves of my chemise three different ways before she was satisfied. To tell the truth, I didn't mind it. When she was done I saw myself in the looking glass and nearly blushed.

At last we issued forth into the watery sunlight in our best things. I wore my red velvet dress with the green underskirt, and Susannah wore a silk dress in two colors of blue and a chemise with pleated sleeves. Joan wore yellow, but her dress was very old.

We took a hackney coach to the theater at Dorset Gardens. It stood on the riverfront, in the gardens of a grand mansion which had burnt in the Great Fire. I had admired the playhouse from without many times, for it was built by Sir Christopher Wren and was very fine. But I had never seen it from within until that day, and I had had no notion of how splendid it would be. Though the afternoon light came but faintly through the windows, the great room was hot and bright with the light of hundreds of wax candles. Some were in sconces, but most hung in rings or chandeliers. The stage came out into the room, and we who were in the audience surrounded it on three sides. Those in the pit sat on benches, and there was much jostling among them, but we were in the eighteen-penny seats and quite comfortable. The Duke of York's coat of arms hung over everything, and his box was just opposite, but he did not come that day. There was a gallery for the musicians, and on either side of that were statues of the Greek muses in glistening stone. When I first entered I drew a quick breath and clasped my fan in my hands, looking all around me. Susannah smiled at my awe, and led us to our seats.

There was an astonishing din. The musicians tuned their instruments, and the girls who sold oranges bawled, "Oranges, oranges, who will buy of me?" The coxcombs who sat in the pit called up to the women who wore vizard masks and tried to flirt with them. Two men quarreled loudly, and an elegant woman in one of the boxes laughed so mightily at something that I feared she would bepiss herself. I tried to venture a remark to Susannah, but could not make myself heard, so at last I gave up and waited in bliss for the play to start and the noise to grow hushed.

But it didn't.

When the musicians first started to play, I thought it had. Certainly it was quieter, or perhaps it only seemed so. The musicians were strange to behold, dressed in taffeta gowns with sleeves trimmed in tinsel. They wore garlands of dried flowers in their hair. The music they played was by turns sweet and lively, and I liked it well, but I was impatient to hear the players speak their parts. At last the fiddlers laid down their bows and then Mr. Betterton himself came onto the stage and opened his mouth to speak the prologue. "We write not now as th'Ancient Poets writ/for your Applause of Nature, Sense and Wit/But like good Tradesmen, what's in fashion vent . . ."

"My husband forbade me to see it," a woman near me

said. "He says Mrs. Behn is brazen to write plays just as though she were a man. Of course he is right. But I could not keep away!" And she giggled.

The other woman answered her, saying her husband had long since given over forbidding her to do things. I stared at them, amazed that they would dare to speak while the play was on. But they were not the only ones. All around me people continued to quarrel, flirt, and chatter. The orange girls cried their oranges and their customers jingled their coins. Indeed, many attended keenly to the business upon the stage, but others paid it no mind at all.

It could not be right. Something was not right.

"Mr. Betterton plays the hero, Wittmore," Susannah said to Joan.

Mr. Betterton bowed, and was clapped, and now two actresses came upon the stage, the first I had ever seen. The clothes they wore were richly colored, and their faces were bright with paint. But what did it matter if I could not hear the lines they spoke, written by the only female playwright in the history of the world?

For a moment I sat in a dark, numb stupor, hearing nothing but the whirl of sound around me. My disappointment was so great that I wanted to cry. But when all around me took it as a matter of course, it seemed too young a thing to do.

Then I was caught by the words "Custom is unkind to our sex, not to allow us free choice." The words trembled in the air near me, and I realized they had come from one of the actresses upon the stage. And I understood that I *could* hear, though it seemed that I could not. As the actresses pranced and rustled in the glow of the foot-candles, their lovely, reckless voices sailed through the hot, bright theater to me.

It was true that I could not hear all. When those near me spoke loudly I often lost a speech, or when the orange girls came by. Once a loud quarrel broke out in the pit, and there were cries of "Duel, duel!" and everyone stood and looked below. I stood, too, though I had seen men duel more than once before in London's streets. But they did not duel, and at last people settled themselves. When I returned my attention to the stage I found I had missed how Lodwick had tricked Sir Credulous, and I was very angry about it, and thought it was pointless to have come to the playhouse. It was better to sit at home and read, after all, where one could get every word. And I vowed I would pay no more mind to the players below, and then I would not care when I missed their speeches.

But it was not so easy, for when I *could* hear I heard in spite of myself, and I caught the laughter of those around me as one catches fleas from another's nearby wig, and soon I felt how charming Wittmore was, and how foolish Sir Credulous, and how sweet Isabella. And despite my vow I soon listened as hard as I could, and leaned forward and cupped my ear with my hand when the conversation near me grew loud. For when the players spoke, a kind of magic happened, and it was as if everything were real indeed, as though I sat and spied through the window upon living people who knew not that I watched.

The play told the story of a rich old merchant, Sir Patient Fancy, who always thought himself ill. He had a young wife who did not love him. There were also two young couples who wanted to marry, but whose parents wanted them to marry others, and many complications of that sort. The players said many funny things, and some clever ones, and there were some very comical moments, most especially when a man was crawling about the floor, and a woman sat down upon him as though he were a footstool, in order to hide him from Sir Patient. At that, Susannah, Joan, and I all laughed heartily.

In the end the lovers married for love, as is the way in happy plays. We all laughed and clapped wildly, and I thought to myself that Aphra Behn was getting money from our merriment, and that made me clap the harder. It seemed a wondrous thing, and for a moment I dreamed of doing it myself.

"Well," Susannah said as we made our way from the theater. "How did you like your first play?"

All my disappointment came back, and I cried out with indignation, "Why do people talk all through it? It is better to sit at home and read the text, I think, for I missed half of what passed!"

She looked at me, and I saw that she was hurt, and that like the players I must act a part, and pretend to feel what I did not.

"That is always the way of it," she answered me after a moment. "But there are some lines in a play like this one it is better not to hear."

"Because it is so bawdy?" I asked her, but just then we emerged into the street.

It had been full daylight when we entered the theater at a little past three, but now it was night, and a light rain was beginning to fall.

"Oh, dear," Joan said. "Well, we won't mind it."

"We must find a coach," Susannah said.

"Look at this! It's hardly dark," I said. It was true, too. Fleet Street was filled with link boys, and each one held a light upon a stick, so that he might earn a few pence guiding the theatergoers through the dark streets. The light from the flames flickered in the puddles that were beginning to form at our feet.

"Pull your hood close," Joan said. "Your hair is getting wet."

I hardly cared. I was not used to being abroad at night, and the excitement of it swept through me as the crowd swept past me. And at that moment I decided that it didn't matter that I had not heard every word said. It did not matter. What mattered was the light dancing in the water, and the memory of bright skirts swishing past the foot-candles, and the lovely, reckless voices sailing, sailing through the dark theater to where we sat with our laughter ready.

"Wasn't it wonderful!" I said. And I was not pretending.

A few days after we saw the play Susannah became very like Sir Patient Fancy, to my mind. She was by nature a cheerful, brisk woman, but now she began complaining frequently. One day she looked in the glass and claimed her eyes were wan, another day she worried that her urine was clouded. She was much bothered by kitchen smells, and said she could not eat. My father was anxious and tender with her, but I saw nothing to be concerned about. I thought perhaps she wanted more attention from my father, who had been very busy of late with the printing of a new sermon by the Dean of Canterbury.

I said as much to Joan, but Joan smiled and shook her head. "Mrs. Moore does not stoop to such stratagems," she said. "She is a plainspoken woman."

I thought about that, and it seemed to me this was true. "Ought I to worry, then? Think you that she is indeed ill?"

"Nay, don't worry," Joan said, smiling more broadly.

So I vowed I would not. But the next morning after breakfast I heard great retchings as I passed through the hall and ran to find Susannah sitting upon the bed, with the bedcurtains drawn back, heaving into a chamber pot.

"You *are* ill," I cried. "The doctor must come."

She waited a moment before she replied, head hanging over the pot, to be sure she was done. Then she set the pot upon the floor and wiped her mouth on the corner of her apron. "No, we need him not."

"Have you the ague?"

"No, no, do not worry."

"Of course I must worry. You may give it to my father, or to me."

Susannah lay back upon the bed as though suddenly she felt weak. "What I have is not contagious," she said with a small smile. "Else every young married woman in London would come to be near me."

Suddenly I understood. "You are breeding," I said.

She nodded. Her eyes were closed, as though she did not want to see my feelings show upon my face. All that I had feared had come to pass. Susannah would bear a child—a son, surely—and I would lose my inheritance. But when I caught a glimpse of my face in the glass, it was not filled with the hatred I thought I felt. What I saw on my face was more like fear. And underneath the thought of my inheritance was the memory of my brother Louis hanging on to my apron with his little hands.

"You must be careful of yourself," I said. "You must rest. I'll call Jane to empty the chamber pot. And perhaps you will want Joan with you?"

She opened her eyes, then, and looked at me, as though she wondered what I was thinking.

"If you please," was all she said, but her eyes followed me as I left the room.

THE MIDWIVES BOOK

O h God, you have sentenced me to get my bread by the sweat of my brows, and my wife to bring forth children in pain and peril. Lord, grant her a gracious delivery, and give her strength to endure it. Though many die in childbirth, may it please you to preserve her life, and the life of the child she bears, that both may be instruments of your glory and vessels of your mercy. Amen."

We sat together in the large parlor: family, servants, apprentices. My father sat in a carved chair and held a Bible on his knees. The curls of his wig swung forward as he bent to peer at the text in the weak firelight. Evening prayers grew longer every day, it seemed to me. My father read chapter upon chapter aloud from Scripture. Sometimes he read an entire sermon. Then he prayed long, and afterward we all chanted psalms together.

"I think my father is more fearful than you are," I said

to Susannah as we left the parlor together one night after he had prayed fervently once more for a gracious delivery.

"Nay," she answered. "He is not."

That made me turn away, for I did not want to know about her fear. I told myself she was only standing up for my father, for she did not act afraid.

The months that Susannah was carrying passed slowly for me. It seemed there were only two topics of conversation in the world: the Papists and my mother's growing belly. Mr. Grove and the Mr. Turners simpered as they asked after her. Neighbor women came often, bringing a gooseberry pie or a pot of jam. They stayed and chattered for hours with Susannah. Sometimes such laughter arose from her chamber that my father and I could hear it in the shop, but he pretended he could not.

On the Feast of St. Valentine I turned thirteen, but no great change occurred. Still I worked in the shop, and read when I could, though I also spent much of my day climbing stairs to wait upon Susannah in her chamber, or in the kitchen stewing things that might tempt my stepmother to eat. Of course she did not go into the shop now, nor into the kitchen, nor to church. My father was by turns merry and cross; he was tender with Susannah and barked at Jane and me when we did not hurry enough upon the stairs. The weather was dreary, with leaden skies and chill winds.

Mrs. Gosse came several times to sit with Susannah, and once she brought Anne. It was on an April afternoon, almost a year after Hester and I had seen the comet in the sky above London. To my great joy, the two of us were given our freedom, and we took our cider and bread into the small parlor where we sat before the glowing coals.

"How lovely that you are to have a brother or sister so soon," Anne began. I sighed before I could help myself, and Anne's eyebrows lifted. "Are you not glad?" she asked.

"Why should I feel glad that my inheritance is to be taken away? It would be better for me if she miscarried." I was sure these words would shock Anne, but I did not care. Speaking them gave me an enormous relief, a sense of freedom. I felt hard and strong all through.

But Anne was not shocked. "Your upbringing has been so odd," she said thoughtfully. "You are not used to the ways of the world. You are always fighting what must be. There can be no peace that way."

"I do not desire peace."

She laughed at that. "Certainly it is not the only prize in life. So, you wish Mrs. Moore to miscarry. Do you think you will get your wish?"

I had not shocked her, but she shocked me. "I did not say I wish it."

"You are of two minds, perhaps. We will judge you by your actions. Do you jostle Mrs. Moore upon the stairs? Do you bring her disagreeable things to eat? Do you drop pewter plates near her that she might be startled by loud noises?"

"You know that I do not. I would not add such a crime to the sins of my soul."

She smiled and lifted her tankard to drink.

"I have mixed tansy and muscatel, and rubbed it into her navel," I said as though making a confession.

"Excellent for preventing miscarriage. I thought as much. You must also protect her from any kind of anxiety or shock. You must not let her have morbid fancies, or indulge in excesses. She must avoid fire, lightning, thunder, and the noise of guns or of great bells. She must not—"

"Look upon monsters lest her child be born deformed," I broke in impatiently. "Nor wind wool, or perhaps her child might strangle in the womb. She must not go to funerals for there might be harmful influences there."

Anne was surprised. "I did not think you would know so much. You have not been near the birth chamber so often as I."

"I read it in Jane Sharp's book for midwives."

"Jane Sharp! My father will not allow her book in the house. He says that it is obscene."

"He would rather that midwives make their deliveries uninstructed, then?"

"You and I are not midwives," she pointed out. "Does your father know you read it?"

I had not thought of this. Probably he did not. But he had never sought to censor my reading in the past. I do not know why I myself bothered to read *The Midwives Book*. I was not interested in women's mysteries. Some girls are drawn to the secrets of the birth chamber from their earliest years; I was not. I had known too much dying

there, perhaps, or maybe it was simply my temperament
to prefer the gossip of men to that of women. And yet I
read Jane Sharp, and read her hungrily, that I might learn
all I could about what was about to pass in our household.

"I have learned from Hester and Joan, as well as Jane
Sharp," I said to Anne.

"Yes, we women always learn from one another. I heard
lately of one lady who ate too many strawberries, and her
child was born with the red mark of the berry upon his
cheek. And there was another woman, who was startled by
a hare bounding across the lane, and she gave birth to a
baby with a hare lip."

This I found most interesting, but I had something to
relate of even greater fascination. "*I* heard of a woman
. . . do not repeat this, I beg of you . . . " I leaned forward
and lowered my voice. "A woman Joan worked for
dreamed of coupling with an Italian man, and when her
baby was born it had dark hair, like an Italian, instead of
the blond hair she and her husband had." I sat back in tri-
umph.

"It cannot be true," Anne said, almost in a whisper.

"Joan herself was there at the birth."

This story impressed Anne greatly, and I felt that I had
come off well, in spite of being younger and less experi-
enced in women's mysteries. It bothered me not that Joan
had made me promise never to tell what I had told Anne.
I had known from the start that I would break the promise
when next I saw Anne Gosse, for what is the good of

knowing a deep secret unless you can share it? As Joan herself knew full well, or she would not have shared it with me.

"I think you will adore your little sister, Meg," Anne said.

"A sister would not be so bad—"

"If it is a brother you will adore him even more."

"I do not think so. A girl would only *share* in my father's fortune when it came time for her dowry, but a boy would take all."

After that day with Anne I thought often about what she had said, and wondered if she was right that I did not wish Susannah to miscarry. Some days it seemed so. Other days it seemed only that I did not wish a miscarriage to be my fault. Wherever the truth lay, I was so careful with her that my father remarked on it one time as we passed on the stairs. He put a hand on my shoulder and gave me such a smile that I could not help but return it. And then I felt badly, as though I had told a lie.

I studied Susannah's face each time I entered her room, for I knew that if she carried a boy it would make her right eye brighter, her right cheek rosier, and her right breast fuller. But I could not see any difference between her right and left sides.

"Has the midwife looked at your urine?" I asked her boldly one day, as I brought her ale and bread and butter while she lay abed. (She had an enormous appetite for bread and butter, and desired to have it several times in a day.)

"Certainly," Susannah replied, tearing greedily at her bread.

"And is it tinged with red, or with white?" I asked.

"She cannot say, not yet." She looked up at me and ceased chewing a moment. "What do you know of such things?"

"Why, it is all in Jane Sharp's book. We sell it in the shop."

"Who is Jane Sharp?"

"She is a midwife who has written a book for midwives."

"Bring it to me, please. I want to read it."

"My father says it is not good for women in your condition to read such things. Do not trouble yourself."

And I took the empty tray away.

My father had said no such thing, of course, but I did not doubt that he would agree with me. I had no doubt, either, that he would like as much as I to know the sex of the child Susannah carried. One day in the shop, when the rain poured down and the customers stayed away, I asked him if he would not consult Mr. Barker about it, but he told me only that it was no concern of mine, and I did not dare to press him.

So it was I who went to Mr. Barker. I pretended to myself that I went to learn the sex of Susannah's child, but it was not that. I knew that he would not tell me, and besides, I had no coin with which to pay him. I think in truth I went to tell him that he was wrong, that I was not the pilot of my craft.

The girl showed me in to the same room in which I had sat before, and soon Mr. Barker came to join me. We stood before each other for a moment in silence. He was all impatience; I was filled with courage and anger.

"Well, what is it, girl?" he asked me sharply.

"I do not know whether you are a good astrologer or a bad one," I answered.

He looked at me with astonishment. "Well, I know that you are an insolent, impudent, immodest girl," he retorted.

"I know," I said, as though it were not very important. "I have tried to change, but I cannot."

"You must ask God for His help," he said gravely.

I nodded politely. It was true I had not tried this expedient, but in my heart I knew this was not a thing God could change. It seemed to me that He Himself had given me my ungovernable tongue, and it seemed doubtful that He could take it away now.

"What difference does it make to you if I am a good or a bad astrologer?" Mr. Barker asked more gently.

"You foretold a great loss in my life, and it came to pass. But you told me I was the pilot of my boat, and I am not. I am not."

"Yes, Margaret, you are. But you are not the ruler of the sea. You cannot control the tides, the currents, the hurricanes. Those you must endure, as must we all." He looked tired when he said it, and I wondered if he was troubled. "Have you steered your boat into the wind, as I bade you?"

I pondered this. "I do not know how."

"When you learn how, things will go easier with you."

"Mr. Barker, can you tell the sex of the child my step-mother carries?"

"I might predict it, if your father asked me to do so— or your mother. But they have not. Ah, Meg, do not look so! Ask me for something I can give you."

At this I lifted my head and said, "Show me your collection, then."

He was surprised for a moment, and I think he debated whether he should once more be offended by my impertinence. But then he smiled broadly. "It is always a pleasure for me to share my treasures with others," he said, and led me to the next room.

It was only another parlor, with stools and tables and a leather chair, but against one wall many shelves had been built, each higher than the next. And each shelf was crowded with strange things. I could not see what sat upon the high shelves, but nearer to my eye there lay a row of long bones.

"Whose bones are these?" I asked.

"This is the bone of a dog," Mr. Barker said, lifting up one that was gray and jagged. He put it down and pointed. "This is from a fox. I do not know whence this came. This is the skull of a cat." He picked up this last and handed it to me.

I stared curiously at the small, hollow bone that sat upon my glove, trying to imagine it with flesh and fur and whiskers. Suddenly I thought of Louis, and handed it back.

"Is everything in your collection dead?" I asked.

"Except those things which never lived. Here I have rocks, some gathered from the countryside, some from the shore. This is a lump of tin, before it has been coined. It is from Cornwall. And this is lead; it is from Derbyshire." I looked curiously at the tin and lead, but they did not look interesting. "This is a Roman coin. It is many hundreds of years old. I bought it from a man who found it in Aldersgate Street."

This I looked at with more interest. It was heavy and square and bore the likeness of a man upon it, even as some half-groats bear the head of King Charles, and some shillings that of King James.

He showed me many things, some everyday, such as lumps of coal, and some strange, such as more coins and pieces of broken pottery. He had shells from faraway islands, and odd carved pieces he said came from Africa. He had many feathers, and a dead bat, and some dead insects. He had a piece of parchment so old I could not read what was writ upon it, which he did not let me touch.

When he had shown me all he led me to his door. "Why do you collect such things?" I asked him before I ventured out upon the Strand.

"When a child is born, he looks first only to his mother. As he grows he learns he has an entire household around him, filled with servants and sweets. Still later he ventures into the streets, and hears the ragman cry, or sees the cocks fight. He learns his letters, his Latin, his arithmetic. Always he is looking beyond himself, and learning. But one day, if he is like most men, he stops. He thinks he has learned all." He smiled at me. "I did not choose to stop, that is all."

☙ 2 ❧

As the weeks passed and Susannah's belly swelled beneath her apron, my father became less merry and more cross. Everyone in the house knew the reason, for nearly every day the argument began anew. Sometimes he pleaded with her, sometimes he commanded her, but to everything he said she replied: "It would not be right, my husband."

Even before she was carrying, Susannah and my father had argued about whether she was to have a wet nurse, but now the argument had grown fierce. "You are my wife and you will do as I bid," he told her, and went scowling about the house and shop. But I doubted that she would.

Of course I was on my stepmother's side in nothing; I could not be. But I knew that if I were she I would feel the same. I do not know if I will ever bear a child, but if I do so I will not send it from me the moment it is born, to be nursed at another woman's breast.

"It would not be right, my husband," she said over and over. She said it calmly, but she said it firmly.

One Sunday afternoon after dinner my stepmother and I sat in the parlor together, I reading, she at her needlework. It was the last day of April, but the rains yet rattled at the windowpanes. Susannah was very restless, and asked me to put a stool nearby that she might put her feet upon it and be more comfortable, and then in five minutes she asked me to remove it, and then to put it back, and so forth. I did all that I was asked politely, and murmured my concern for her. My concern was neither felt nor feigned, it was in some strange middle-land. I told myself that I wanted her to miscarry, yet I also worried sometimes that I might bring the child harm because I did not welcome it.

The fourth time I moved the stool for her she said, "I am sorry to bother you so."

" 'Tis no bother."

"Yes, it is a monstrous bother, but you bear it well. You are careful of your brother or sister."

I began to read again, for I did not like to hear false praises. Then I looked up. "Jane Sharp says that you ought to wear an eagle-stone. A stone within a stone, you know, it is like the babe within you. If you wear it round your neck, so as to touch your skin, it will keep you from miscarrying."

Susannah smiled faintly. "Yes, I have heard that some believe that."

"They are from Africa, but I know they are to be had in London. Why do you not ask my father to buy you one? Jane Sharp is a wise midwife."

"I will do so, if it pleases you."

We heard the outside door then, and straightened up in expectation, for my father had gone out directly after dinner but said he would speak with Susannah immediately when he came home. Now he brought into the parlor a smiling, big-bellied woman with rosy cheeks.

"This is Mrs. Walker," he said. "Her babe will come two months before yours, so she will have her strength back before she begins to nurse your child. She lives in Broad Street, so the babe will not be in the country, but close by, and can be brought to you often. This much I do for you."

I looked at Susannah, waiting for her to say in her calm way, "It would not be right, my husband." But she did not, and I could see that she was too tired to argue it more. Her face was pale and her eyes were shadowed with her weariness. She lifted her head as though to speak, but then dropped it again. Her hands lay still on her needlework.

I do not know why I did what I did next. Perhaps because I thought of Louis, happy sucking at my mother's breast, and thinking of him could not do otherwise. But later that afternoon when my father was out, I searched through the shop and collected all the texts I could find to support a woman nursing her own child. Jane Sharp wrote that sending a child to a wet nurse would change its disposition and expose it to many hazards. Robert Cleaver wrote that it would "break the bond of holy nature," but he was a Puritan and I did not know if my father would heed his words overmuch. I was glad now to have read *The Ladies' Calling*, though it had given me such pain, for I thought Dr. Allestree's arguments might be the most persuasive with my father. He wrote that women of wealth and rank do not lower themselves in nursing their own children, because a baby takes its rank from its mother and is exactly equal to her, whether she be beggar or gentle-woman.

I gathered together all these works and laid them out upon my father's table in the large parlor, one next to the other. Then I waited to see what he might say.

The following morning all the works were back in the shop, but I knew not how my father had taken my interference, for he said nothing. But at dinner that day, he said to Susannah, "I have told Mrs. Walker we shall not need her services."

Bright color came into my stepmother's cheeks, and she set her tankard quickly down on the table.

"A man must look beyond fashion," my father continued. "And it is the opinion of many that a child's welfare is best protected at the breast of his own mother. You ought to have showed me those texts before, my wife."

"Texts?" she asked in surprise, and then everyone's gaze seemed to shift about the table. I could feel Susannah looking at me, and back at my father, and my father sat back in uncertainty. I laced my fingers tightly together and stared into my dinner plate, where a scrap of roast beef, covered with pepper and vinegar, was all that remained of my dinner. I knew he would be severe upon me if he discovered my meddling.

"Did you not put works upon my table for me to read?" my father asked.

"Yes, of course," Susannah answered. "For I know you to be a just and a thoughtful man, who heeds the advice of fine writers."

Carefully, I took my spoon once more into my hand.

"Husband," Susannah said. "Jane Sharp advises a woman who is breeding to wear an eagle-stone around her neck. Can you get one for me?"

❧ 3 ❧

Susannah's confinement came at midsummer. As it approached she became every day more fretful and more afraid. She no longer came to evening prayers, or even to dinner, and I made countless trips up and down the stairs with the chamber pot, for she seemed to use it a hundred times within an hour.

One day, but two weeks before she delivered, she caught my hand as I was taking away the tankard in which she had drunk sage ale (to strengthen her womb). "Margaret, listen to me," she said sharply.

I paused, surprised.

"I know you do not welcome my child," she said, letting her hand drop. "But you do not consider how pleasing it may be to have children near. You had brothers and sisters once before, was it so terrible a thing?"

"No," I said, nearly whispering. There was much more I could have said to her, but I did not say it.

"It does not matter. You have attended me well in spite of it all, more than well. I am not ungrateful. But I want something more of you."

I felt weary all through, thinking that all I had done for

her these past months had not been enough. "What more, Mother?" I asked quietly.

"If I die, and my child lives, you must care for it. You must protect it, you must argue for it. Make your father school it well, in Greek and Latin if it is a boy, in household arts if it is a girl. Show my child a woman's love. You are young to be a mother, but I want my baby to be raised in his father's house. Promise me, Margaret. I will trust your promise."

I stood very still for a moment, with her empty tankard yet in my hand. "You worry overmuch," I said at last. "All will be well."

"Do you refuse to promise, then?"

Her look was almost woeful, and I turned my eyes away, and fingered the green velvet bed hangings with my free hand. "No," I said in a low voice. "I do not refuse it."

"If I die, you will be mother to my child?"

"I will be its mother."

"Ah." She lay back upon her pillows. "Now I shall not worry."

Of course I did not want to be a mother. I wanted to be a bookseller, perhaps even an author someday. I told myself I would not mind being some man's helpmeet in fair partnership, if I liked him, or an independent woman who made my own way, like Aphra Behn. But for the time being I wanted only to be a girl, helping her father at the sign of the Star.

I promised in spite of myself, though, because of Louis.

All was now ready for the birth. We had prepared a sheet for the lying-in, an abundance of swaddling clothes, and mantles, all of finest linen. The window in the birth chamber was covered with a tapestry, that the room might stay warm and dark, like the womb itself. There was a board for Susannah to brace her feet against, and a velvet cord for her to hang on to when the pain became great.

I did not like to think of that. I remembered the howls of my own mother sounding through the house. I did not want to hear such screams again.

My father felt the same, and when the time came, he did all that a father must do for his wife, and then left for Will's. I was not so lucky. Though I did not enter the birth chamber, because of my youth, I was kept busy running up and down the stairs with caudles and ale for the women within. There were the two midwives, who had seen Susannah throughout her pregnancy, Susannah's older sister, who had herself delivered but three months past and came with her baby in her arms, two cousins, Mrs. Gosse (but not Anne), and the nurse. The midwives brought stools, knives, sponges, and oil of lilies which they used upon their hands; I knew this from reading Jane Sharp. But I did not see them use it, nor did I see Susannah under her splendid linen sheet. I only passed things through a crack of the door and listened.

At first there was much laughter and chatter, as though at a party, and sometimes the baby cried. But as the hours passed the voices lowered, and sometimes I heard Susannah groaning, or crying out. Once I heard her say breathlessly, "God, help me to bear it!" After that I hid myself in the farthest corner of the house and read tales of Robin Hood and imagined myself far from London, in Sherwood Forest. I let the nurse do the fetching, and tried not to hear her footsteps upon the stairs, but heard them anyway. Once I followed her into the kitchen in spite of myself and asked: "How does it go?"

"Don't worry," the nurse said kindly. "We are only waiting upon nature."

Then I went back to my book but I read it not; instead I prayed to God, as my father had done, for a swift and easy delivery.

My prayers were granted. Late that night, so late that the laundresses had begun to rattle their tubs next door, Tobias William Moore was born, and became my father's heir.

❧ 4 ❧

And now there was nothing more that could be done. My last chance was gone. I had done all I could, all that was within God's law, to preserve my inheritance, but I had failed. I knew now that my hopes were finally dashed, and that my future would not be different from that of other women.

But I had a brother again.

I do not mean to say it was enough. I do not mean to say I would have chosen it. But when I held his swaddled body in my arms, and saw the curl of his reddened fingers, I could not help but love him. "Toby," I called him. I was the first to call him so, but soon we all did.

Susannah suckled him herself, and when she did so, the peace upon her face made its way into my father's heart, and he said, "I have chosen well."

I supposed that I would have much hard work during those first weeks, but the truth was I did not wait upon Toby even as often as I wanted. He slept much, and when he did not Susannah wanted him near, or the nurse held him, and even my father wanted his turn. And there were many gossips about—the same women who visited Susannah while she was breeding and who were in her chamber during the birth. So there was little for me to do in the house, and I began more and more to work in the shop again. I was glad enough to be back when it was busy, but sometimes, when I had no one to wait upon, and the dusting was done and every book sat with straightened pages, I stared through the window at the grass growing in the ruts of the road and thought about my chances.

I was not an heiress any longer. I would not have my pick of suitors; I could not tell all but booksellers to take themselves off. Most likely I would be married to some other sort of tradesman, a draper or a goldsmith or a barber, a widower with children of his own, perhaps. Most likely.

But the things that are most likely do not always come to pass.

I thought of this, and clasped my hands together, and tried to imagine other futures.

"What are you thinking about that makes your face so fierce?" Mr. Winter asked me as he came into the shop.

I gave my head a shake, and he saw I did not want to answer.

"I have never seen you sit and think; you are always reading when I come, unless you are working," he continued.

"I have decided to leave off reading and begin writing instead. I am composing a play."

"Well done!" Mr. Winter said. "I would be most honored to see it when you are ready for readers."

I did not know how to answer him, for I had spoken in jest. But it's true that since seeing Mrs. Behn's play it had been much on my mind to try my hand, and perhaps that longing made my frivolous words seem serious. Now I was too embarrassed to explain myself, and only mumbled that it would be a good while, and then we spoke of Toby, and Susannah's health.

But when next alone I found paper and quill, and began to write down the scraps of speech that had been living so unwelcome in my head these past months, as rats do in a kitchen.

At first these scraps made themselves into rhymes. I had lived long with the music of Mr. Dryden's couplets in my head, and had many times heard him speak of the nobility of this form. I, too, wanted to write noble speeches, even if they would never be uttered. My rhymes trailed down the page, and I read them over with pleasure, and waited eagerly for the moment I would be alone and could read them aloud. But when it came at last, my words did not sound noble at all, only foolish.

I threw my paper in the fire, and for an angry week I did not write. But once again I found myself haunted by phrases. This time they were not noble, and they did not rhyme. And so I came to know that in spite of all I had learned from him, I could not be a follower of John Dryden, but must instead take my lead from Mrs. Behn.

In my scene a man lectured his wife on philosophy, while his wife nodded and agreed and showed him how to use a fork, and how to clean his teeth, and to do all the everyday things a woman knows better than a man how to do. As I wrote it I thought it very droll, and longed to hear another person laugh at it, but when I read it over I thought it childish, and was sure no other person on earth could find amusement in it. It felt so bold even to have written it that I thought I could never show it to Mr. Winter, and decided I would tell him it had all been a jest, and I had nothing to show. Yet when I had finished, and it was as ready as I could make it for the eyes of another, it vexed me that he did not come into the shop for four days running.

At last, however, he came again. The moment I saw him I felt my stomach dancing within me, and knew at once that I must give him the scene even if I did not want to.

He spoke first to my father, for a man they both knew had been robbed by highwaymen as he rode in a coach, and had lost his money and jewelry.

"No one was hurt, thank God," Mr. Winter said.

My father and I exclaimed in dismay, and my father said soberly, "It is growing unsafe to travel through our own countryside."

Mr. Winter shrugged. "Life has never been safe. Read Thucydides. Read Shakespeare. For whom has it ever been safe?"

Just then Mr. Dodds came in. He was an old man who read much and always brought us his trade. He began to speak with my father about political subjects, and I was grateful, for I could not speak to Mr. Winter of my play with my father listening.

"I have something for you," I said in a low, hurried voice as he turned to me.

He looked startled at first, and I saw that he had forgotten our conversation. But then remembrance dawned on his face, and, with a glance at my father to see that he was unobserved, he reached for the roll of paper I held out to him.

Almost three weeks now had passed since my brother came into the world, and it was nearly time for Susannah's upsitting. She was most anxious for it, feeling quite well again and ready to go once more into London's streets. My father was uneasy at first, for my mother had never been ready for her upsitting before a month had passed. But Susannah did not look as my mother was used to look, wan and tired all the day though she did nothing but lie abed. Susannah's cheeks were pink, and her face filled with delight when she held her child, and she seemed full of vigor. So my father gave in, and began to ask instead what he ought to serve at the gossips' supper.

On the day of the upsitting the gossips came early, and threw away the soiled linens from my mother's bed, and bathed her, and dressed her in petticoats and a blue dress with a rose-colored underskirt. One of the women clicked her tongue and said her stays did not lace as tightly as before, and said that was what came of nursing her own child. But Susannah laughed and said she did not care. She asked me if I would brush her hair for her, and I did, though another woman dressed it. And then we went below for the supper: hare pie, and much wine. I think I had never before seen so many merry women. They toasted the King's health, and my mother's, and my father's, and of course Toby's. And then they toasted mine.

"And that she might marry well!" one woman said loudly. "A silversmith, perhaps!"

"Nay," Susannah said, smiling. "Meg will marry a bookseller." She looked at me hard when she said it, harder than she ever had when she was teaching me to candy violets or to work a chair cover. I knew that it was not something that was within her power to promise, but in spite of myself I thought: Maybe it will come to pass after all.

They lifted their tankards, and drank my health.

It was the next day that Mr. Winter came once more into the shop. He did not speak to me, but addressed my father, and a sick feeling went all through me, for I knew he avoided me because my work was so bad, or perhaps because he had not cared to read it. I busied myself at my counter and tried not to listen, but I could not help hearing them as they spoke of what Mr. Greene had said of Mr. White, and of whether the Duke of York's bride could give him an heir, and of the plays given in Dorset Gardens and Drury Lane.

And then I heard Mr. Winter say: "I have read something very fine lately, something very witty and droll, but you cannot read it, for it is yet in manuscript."

"Who will publish it?" my father asked.

"Why, no one, yet. A friend of mine has written it. It is a play, or a part of a play, and as good as some things I have seen the King's Company perform."

"Why does your friend not finish it?"

"Oh, she will, or she will write something else as good. She will write when she is ready. She is young yet, and has things to learn, but she will have us all laughing at her plays someday if she chooses."

"Another she-poet! One Aphra Behn is enough, I think," my father said.

"All women may write plays as far as I am concerned, if they write as well as Aphra Behn," Mr. Winter answered him. Then he turned to smile at me. My face was scarlet. I knew he spoke of my work, yet I could hardly believe he meant the things he said, and I was glad he left without a private word.

But the rest of the day the air was changed. It was light and fresh, and my thoughts were light and fresh. Each printed page smelt of promise and possibility. And I thought about my future and for the first time I believed it to be yet unwritten.

Perhaps I will marry a bookseller.

Perhaps I will be a cherished member of my brother Toby's household.

Perhaps Toby will yet die (though I do not wish it) and I will be an heiress once more.

Perhaps I will make my fortune writing plays, like Aphra Behn. Perhaps.

We do not know our futures, though we sometimes think we do. The world is full of strange things and strange chances. There is no safety, but neither can we be certain that any given sorrow will be ours, not until it comes upon us.

We do not know what every comet means.

What is there to do in this life, then, but to choose as Mr. Barker has chosen? To be open to all, to go on learning, to steer one's boat into the wind?

And this is what I mean to do from this day, one day after another, at the sign of the Star.

AUTHOR'S NOTE

The major characters in this book—the ones you hear talking, quarreling, and laughing—are fictional. I invented Meg and her entire family, including Miles Moore, bookseller. I also made up Anne Gosse and her family, Meg's neighbors, customers such as Paul Winter, and publishers such as Mr. Fletcher. I created Mr. Barker, the astrologer, and his almanac; I also created Mr. Pennyman and *A Wife's Misdeeds*.

But most of the authors mentioned really existed during the years in which my story is set. Each book that serves as a chapter title was a real book written by a real author of the time. The astrological prognostications from *News from the Stars* really were taken from that book, which I read on microfilm, and Hannah Woolley's recipes really were used during the seventeenth century. The only liberty I took was with the book *An Antidote Against Melancholy*. Although copies of this book still exist, none was accessible to me when I was doing my research. I liked the title so much that I used it anyway, and took the verses Meg refers to from a book called *Samuel Pepys' Penny Merriments*, edited by Roger Thompson.

According to this source, the song between Nanny and Jenny, called "New London Drollery," was printed in 1687, and the riddle Meg tells Paul Winter is from "Merry Riddles," which was published in 1685.

Of the authors whose books serve as chapter titles, Aphra Behn (1640–1688) deserves special mention, because it surprises many today to learn that a successful female playwright lived more than three hundred years ago. And Aphra Behn was indeed successful. Between 1670 and 1688 over a dozen of her plays were staged in London, and only John Dryden had more plays produced at court for the royal family. Behn's success presumably encouraged other women to try their hands at playwriting. In the 1690s (when Meg would have been in her thirties) Catherine Trotter, Mary de la Rivière Manley, and Mary Pix all had their works produced in London's playhouses.

Those interested in learning more about these women playwrights, or in reading the plays they wrote, should consult *The Female Wits*, by Fidelis Morgan.

Readers who want to find out more about the period might enjoy Liza Picard's *Restoration London*, and those who share my special interest in how women fared at the time may wish to read Antonia Fraser's *The Weaker Vessel*, which deals with the varied roles of English women throughout the seventeenth century.

Many people helped this book come into being, sometimes without even knowing it (such as the countless librarians who helped me find my way to sources). I would like especially to thank Carol Dorf, Larry Holben, Marian Michener, Lee Sturtevant, and Peter Szego for reading the work in manuscript; the women in my writing group for their suggestions and support; Wesley Adams, my editor at Farrar, Straus & Giroux; and the people who keep me going: Andrea Goodman, Larry Holben, and Ron.